Wynter 2

An Ice-Cold Love

Trenae'

Trenae' Presents

Contents

Dedication

This book is dedicated to my heart and my headache, Ava Marie. There's no limit to what I would do to make sure there is always a smile on your face, gorgeous. Anything I do is for my light bright god-child. Nanny loves you and will move heaven and earth to make you smile.

To my sister, Asia Lewis, we the girls of the crew and swear we stay live! I can't thank you enough for giving me the opportunity to know and love Ava! Love ya gah.

To my brother, Kevin Lewis Jr. My giant I'm so proud of you for following your dreams and never giving up. You went to college and dominated the court as well as those classes and graduation is coming up. Love you my big lil brother.

Acknowledgments:

Fourteenth book Shawtttttyyy!!!! Lol
This part never gets easy because of course
I don't want to miss anyone. First and foremost,
I want to thank God for giving me the gift of
storytelling. I'm still shocked that I can actually
create a story that you, my readers, love. It
baffles me that I went through so much schooling
just to end up coming back to what I've always
loved, writing. I know that that was no one but
God's doing. Without him, there would be no
Trenae' and for that I am forever grateful.

To my fiance' and best friend, Joe. You are
the most supportive man a girl could ask for. You
accept when I can't pay attention to you because
I'm chasing the bag, you motivate me when I feel
like giving up, you allow me to bounce ideas off of
you and you even throw out titles. (Even if they suck
and I never use them lol). I love you because even
when I'm a mess, you love me. When I'm working on
a book, I know I look a mess on the regular, but you
still tell me I'm the prettiest girl ever. I'm grateful
for the times you start meals and clean the kitchen
so that I can work. You are an amazing man and

an amazing father. I love you forever and a day and I can't wait to say I do, over and over again.

To my parents, Trudy, Keith and Tarunye thank you for the continued support. As soon as I say my book is live y'all quickly one-click and I definitely appreciate it.

To the women who played a huge role in raising me, my grandmother Deloris, my aunt Betty and my aunt Mona, I appreciate every sacrifice you made to make sure I never went without anything I needed. Thank you for all that y'all do.

To my siblings, Kevin, Malika, Asia, Tarya, Makia, Jayanma and Zuri, I love y'all and never forget that the sky is the limit.

To my Godchild and constant headache, Ava, anything that I do is for you! It's my job to make sure that smile never falls from your face and I'll work overtime to make sure that happens. Nanny loves you forever and a day Phat-Phat!

To my cousins that are more like siblings, Raquel, Reggie, Trevor and Boots I love y'all!

To my squuuuuaaaaddddd lol, Chrissy, Fantasia and Kelleashia bruh so many of y'all stories find their way into my books. My characters are based off of y'all and everything, thanks for the constant laughs. Above all that thanks for remaining the same, y'all never switched up on the kid and I appreciate that. You know y'all stuck with me foreva (Cardi B voice).

Keondria, Secret, Kelleashia, and Rikida, I can't thank y'all enough for the brutal honesty y'all give me. Y'all been rocking with me since The Sins of Beretta one and long after I have ended their story here you are all, still by my side. Y'all the best!

B Capri "Cardi B" Miller, my boo thang, you know there is nothing but love between us. In you, I found not only a friend but a sister. And I got my brother AJ! LOL! You are such a beautiful person on the inside and that is complemented by your outer appearance. From the moment we spoke we just clicked! You motivate me to write when all I want to do is watch the firestick! When I have no more ideas to give, you throw random shit out. You stuck with me foreva!

Coco Shawnde, my black barbie and one of my best friends. You are one of the most hard - working women that I personally know. There isn't a day that goes by that you don't inspire me. You've went from being someone that I spoke with from time to time to being family. I love how caring, goofy and motivating you are. Plus, you love Gates so you gotta be lit. I pray that your season for winning in this industry is near! You are dope and baby they have to stop sleeping on you soon.

Junk in the trunk, (DEDRA) the pretty pen pusha herself. Looking at you, no one would know your past struggle and that's the beauty I see in it. You always have a smile on your face and a curse word on your tongue for me. (Killing myself laughing!) I love that the industry is finally seeing you for the dope author you are. It's your time baby, shine!

Secret, my friend and my editor. My books wouldn't be anything without your help and suggestions. I appreciate you for first being a loyal test reader then an amazing editor. Besides that, your friendship means the world to me! I love you even when you answer facetime with one lash and Meek Mill braids. Kmsl!

To my sisters of KBC thanks for y'all continued support, Love y'all.

Last but most certainly not least, to YOU my readers, I cannot thank you all enough for continuing to rock with me. Y'all took a chance on a new author and been rocking with me since! I will strive to never let y'all down. Thanks for the inboxes and reviews on my past work, I definitely took everything y'all said into consideration. I have to also thank y'all for being patient with me, as I got this book done for you all.

If I missed anyone, know that it wasn't intentional. Charge my memory and not my heart for that mistake. I hope you enjoy my new series because these characters took me for a ride and never stopped talking to me!

Want to keep up with Trenae'?
Facebook: Paree Trenae
Facebook: Author Trenae'
Instagram: Trenaedhaplug
Twitter: Ooh_Paree_Dear
Snapchat: PareeTrenae
Periscope: PareeTrenae
Add my reader's group: Trenae'
Presents: The Juice

Synopsis:

What is one to do when the man she saw herself spending forever with shows her time and time again that she isn't enough? Entering her final days of pregnancy, Wynter has never felt more alone in this world. With her past and her present colliding in an emotional explosion, she has no clue of what her future holds. At one point, she saw her future in Supreme's eyes, but his lies and betrayals have turned something that was once crystal clear, into a ball of questions and confusion. Whenever doubt and a lack of trust is brought into a relationship, it leaves the door open for outsiders to enter. In his usual cocky fashion, Ice waltzes right on in ready to stake claim on his wife and the baby he had no hand in creating. What he didn't expect was for the Wynter he once knew, to no longer exist. Though her new attitude proved to be a problem, Ice would stop at nothing to get what was rightfully his. If dealing with a two-way love affair isn't complicated enough, piling on the relationship problems of her sister and best friend may just be Wynter's breaking point. In this finale, lies will be revealed and secrets will be spilled. Will Wynter get the happily ever after she deserves or are fairytales only reserved for the girls who never venture to the hood?

Where we left off...

Wynter

"Get your ass out the bed man." I heard right before I felt the stinging sensation of Supreme's hand slapping against my bare ass.

"Go on, Supreme, leave me alone ugly ass lil boy." I said with my face buried in the pillow. "That key is supposed to be used in case of an emergency."

"You know ain't shit about a nigga ugly Wynter. And this was an emergency, I needed to make sure wasn't nobody in this bitch. Wake your ass up so that these people can come help you get ready for today. It's already 12." He said smacking my ass again and then making his exit. I laid around for a few moments longer before finally climbing out the bed. I rubbed my stomach and talked to my baby girl as I made my way to the bathroom where Supreme had ran my bath water. Watching the steam rise from the tub let me know that he ran it just like I loved it, steaming hot. The bubble bath and bath bombs, he used smelled amazing, so I happily submerged my swollen body into the tub and hit the buttons for the jets to turn on. Laying my head back, I couldn't help but to pray. Not to ask for anything, but to thank God for everything. I was in a real dark place and to be honest, I didn't think I would find my way out of it. By the grace of God, I did.

"You think I should give your daddy a second chance?" I asked Rhea and her ass kicked. That kick could be a hell no or it could be a go for it. Supreme had been amazing throughout this pregnancy and hasn't pressured me into dropping the whole friendship situation. I was able to start all over and learn him even better than I did to begin with. In five months I never saw him aggravated with how slow we were moving. He had even started coming to counseling sessions with me, so he was able to know me a lil better also.

"Wynter?" I heard Koko call out as she walked into the bedroom then entered the bathroom "Supreme sent me to wake your ass up. He said you were being lazy." She laughed as I rolled my eyes.

"Tell his ugly ass, I was being pregnant. I'm so tired Koko, do I have to go to this shower? I don't think this lil girl needs anything else, the nursery is full already." I whined.

"Well, no one told you to start shopping. You knew we were planning this shower ages ago so, good thing you have two other rooms available for the overflow. Now get your ass out of the bathtub so that we can start making you pretty." She said walking out.

"Soooo, what you saying is I'm not pretty now?" I asked.

"Exactly." She said laughing and making her exit.

"WHORE!" I screamed at her back as we both laughed. I was appreciative to Koko for all she had done with this shower, so I wouldn't complain too much. Washing off, I stepped out the tub and handled the rest of my personal hygiene, before grabbing a robe and heading down stairs. My living room was transformed into a full-service salon as the travel spa Supreme ordered set everything up for me. I was so happy at this very moment that my emotional ass started crying. Not big boo hoo tears, just a few here and there. A few hours later, I stood in front of the mirror looking and feeling like a million bucks. I wasn't even dressed yet but that didn't matter to me, hell I was sexier naked anyway. My hair and makeup was flawless. I loved that the stylist took my theme into consideration. Because I was naming my daughter Rhea, I decided to go with a Greek goddess themed shower. My hair was blown out, then curled and held in place by a headband that looked like gold wings or feathers. My makeup was tastefully and subtly done and allowed my natural beauty to shine through. The gown I was wearing today was long, white and flowy. The sleeves on the gown were sheer and the gold accessories really completed the look. I had no idea where Supreme went but he told me that a car was coming to get me in thirty minutes. The shower was set to begin in the next fifteen minutes and although I complained, I was now excited.

"Really Wynter, you still aren't dressed?" Rayne asked walking in and shaking her head. Without another word, she lifted the dress and slid it over my head, making sure it didn't touch the makeup on my face.

"I can't believe I'm about to be someone's parent Rayne." I said filled with so much joy.

"Well believe it! Let's go, the car is here." She said as I slid my feet into the gold slippers and grabbed my clutch. "Wynter, we don't know many people so, why did Supreme get a huge venue?" She asked.

"His family and friends. I'm really nervous about that more than anything. Oh, and a lot of his business partners are supposed to be coming. Chile, this shower is more for him than it is for Rhea and I." I laughed at my joke, but the truth was I really didn't care. I was here for the food. As we arrived to the venue, my mouth fell open. I could only imagine what the inside looked like because the outside was breathtaking. I had no say so in anything that had to do with the shower but my theme. Everything else was left up to Supreme. So far, I was impressed. Stepping out of the car I started to the front door before I notice that Rayne wasn't behind me. Looking back, I noticed that she was talking on the phone, so I left her to have some privacy. Supreme must have been watching the door for when I arrived because I was barely in the building when he came over to me.

"Ma, you look so beautiful." He said looking amazed.

"I feel beautiful, thanks. Supreme, I'm nervous, I don't know half of these people." I whispered.

"You good, I'm right here with you." He said guiding me into the room as everyone clapped at my entrance. I had never been to a baby shower, so I didn't know what was next. Luckily, I didn't have to wait long because Koko stepped out.

"Hey again everyone, the mommy to be is here so we can actually start. As you've noticed, I have given each of you a clothes pin. This is a part of the game that will be going on throughout the entire event. Once I say go, no one is allowed to say the word baby. If you here someone saying the word, you may collect their clothes pin. The person with the most at the end of the shower wins." She announced, and I thought it was cute that the men were actually participating. While she continued on with the next game I waved Supreme over.

"You good?" He asked.

"I am, but your daughter isn't. We hungry." I said pouting. I know that we were supposed to wait for the games to pause so that everyone could eat but, everyone wasn't carrying a baby. I was starving, and the food smelled amazing.

"It's not time to eat." Koko said walking over at the same time as Supreme.

"But, I'm hungry Koko." I whined.

"Ok, don't cry to me when you can't drop the baby weight," She said making my mouth fall open.

"Take it back, bitch!" I spat causing her to laugh.

"Leaver her alone Koko. If she wants to eat she can eat, this her shit anyway." Supreme said, taking up for me.

"Your ass just taking up for her because you think its going help you get back in the door." Koko clowned flicking him off and going to host the next game.

"Let me find out that's why you're being so nice to me." I teased him while eating a chicken salad sandwich.

"Nah, you gassing it. I'm going always be nice to you, you are my fucking heart. You about to have my baby and you going make me the happiest woman alive." He said.

"Well, I appreciate the efforts you've been putting in. It doesn't go unnoticed." I said before pulling him close. "So, are you coming home tonight and take care of my needs?" I asked licking his ear. These damn pregnancy hormones were no joke. I already had a high sex drive, now my ass was horny eighty-five percent of the day.

"Home?" He asked with a huge smile on his face.

"Home. It's time, make sure are your closets are empty and you done with those hoes." I said feeding him some of the fettucine he had piled on my plate.

"Ain't no hoes ma, I haven't looked at another chick since you left me. Scout's honor." He said staring me in the eyes.

"Alright Supreme, I'll trust you with my heart one more time. Play with it and see. It took a lot for me to get over all the hurt, I'm not going back there! Your ass will end up in a body bag before I end up there again." I snapped.

"Well, ain't this awkward." A lady who I knew was his mama said walking up with Shoota. "If you kill my baby, who will come visit me on Sunday's when I cook?" She asked laughing.

"I'll visit you on Sunday's and even cook one Sunday out the month." I offered.

"Oh, girl let me go get my gun so you can kill his ass." She said laughing. "We haven't been formally introduced but I'm Ella Mae, and unfortunately I'm their mama." She said making me laugh. I realized in that moment, I hadn't seen Rayne.

"Nice meeting you, I'm Wynter." I said hugging her. "Shoota, you saw Rayne outside?" I asked.

"Yeah, her and that fuck boy out there arguing and shit. Where the food at?" He asked changing the subject. Rayne had really hurt him and I don't think she realized just how much.

"You are glowing, how are you enjoying these last few moments as a pregnant woman?" Ms Ella asked.

"I enjoyed it, but like that old school song said, the thrill is gone." I said making us both laugh. "I'm blessed because some women aren't able to carry their own kids but baby, I'm ready for my own body back." I truthfully answered.

"I understand that. I have to say, you make it look like a walk in the park." She complimented me as Koko appeared from out of nowhere. She took the plate I was still holding on to and made sure my hair was in place.

"What's going on?" I asked. "Is it time for pictures?"

"Uhhh, Yeah something like that." She vaguely answered as the lights dimmed. When I heard the song, Love Don't Change play tears flooded my eyes. This was our song. A projector came on and I was met with a slideshow of pictures and videos. There were some of Supreme and I, us and the girls, me and the girls and some of just myself. I laughed when the video of the girls and I doing his makeup while he was sleeping appeared. Suddenly, the screen went black and it said, "Wait there's more..." The music changed and the Jagged Edge remix of Let's Get Married started playing. All the people that I thought knew Supreme, stood to their feet and started performing. I was a complete mess by the time they were finished and turning around and seeing Supreme down on one knee didn't help.

"Babe, what are you doing?" I asked in total shock.

"Wynter, I lost you once and can't allow that to happen again. You are my entire heart and my soul. I love you, my girls love you and we would really love it if you married us." My words were stuck in my throat when he opened the box on the biggest most exquisite diamond I had ever seen. My mind ran over the what if's and I even thought of Ice. Not even that could stop me from accepting this ring and this man. Before I could answer the projector showcases the "wait, there's more..." again and even Supreme looked confused. Moments later, the high I was just on disappeared and my heart shattered. On the screen was a video of Supreme fucking Makayla for everyone to see and hear.

"Supreme... how could you?" I asked as tears fell from my eyes.

"Nah, somebody fucking with me! This shit old bae." He tried to explain.

"And there you go, lying again. You just got that tattoo Supreme. I hate your punk ass! Why beg me to come back? Why take me through all the motions if you just keep running back to that free before eleven ass hoe. I'm glad I see the real you, you can have that ring my nigga cause no I don't accept your proposal. Matter of fact, you ain't got to worry about Wynter again." I said still talking over the moaning that was going on.

"Supreme you foul for this one my nigga!" Koko spat.

"Nah, he ain't do shit wrong. He was just being plain ole Supreme. A greedy nigga, he had his cake but needed the ice cream too. I'm out!" I said making my way to the door before my past barged in.

"I've only been to one baby shower in my life, but I don't remember the entertainment being that live." Isaiah said laughing at the porn playing in the background.

"Say fam, who the fuck are you?" Shoota asked with his hand at his hip. I knew his gun was resting there. As if on cue, men entered the room with their guns drawn. I shook my head when I saw Brandon standing amongst them. That nigga had eyes on us the whole time. The rest, I recognized them because they were Isaiah's crew from back home.

"This ain't that, lil curly haired bitch." Isaiah told Shoota, who didn't give a fuck about the other guns drawn as he pulled his own out. Supreme was right on side of him with his two out also.

"Oh I got yo curly haired bitch." He said mugging Isaiah.

"Nah, you had my curly haired bitch while I was locked down but playtime is over. Wynter, Rayne is waiting in the car for you." Isaiah said. I knew he was only saying the part about Rayne to force me to go. Little did he know, I was ready before he showed up.

"Wynter you ain't got to go nowhere, I'll go get Rayne out that fucking car if you say the word." Supreme said making me laugh.

"Oh, now you want to protect me. I don't need protection from him, I know what to expect when I'm with him. You, you the person I need protection from." I said walking towards Isaiah. When I got close enough, he pulled me in his arms and I didn't resist. In fact, I pulled his face closer and kissed him with so much passion I felt his dick rock up. "Oh Supreme, I couldn't marry you anyway. Three years ago, I said I do and ain't shit changed. Like I said, I know what I'm getting from my husband, your ass is a toss up." I said walking out.

"Well, y'all enjoy the rest of the festivities." Isaiah said following me out as his men stayed behind.

"Aye Ice, you want us to grab these gifts." One called out.

"You can take it to ya'll kids if ya'll want to. My child won't ever touch that shit!" He spat out starring at Supreme. I saw all kinds of emotions displayed on his face but fuck him. He ain't care about my feelings and I was damn sure done with caring about his. On my way out, I hugged Koko and promised to be in touch soon. I didn't know what my next move was, I just knew it wouldn't be here with Supreme's scandalous ass.

Now, the drama continues in this finale...

Chapter 1:

Supreme

I was stupid, really stupid. Something told me deep inside better not do it.

What a dummy, such a dummy, to let some mess I shouldn't did take you from me. Girl if I could take it back, it'd be so back. I'd be such an angel, you'd think that me and Jesus was cool. Like that, just like that, everything between us be good. Girl I know what I should have done. Should have walked away the moment that I saw her coming. But I blew it, really blew it. And lost the only girl I love. Dear God if you're listening now, I need you do a thing for me. You see my baby, she done up and walked out. I need you bring her back to me. I know that I was wrong, I was guilty in sin and I'm probably not priority. But dear God if you're listening now. I'm down here, dying, begging, crying. Somebody needs to pray for me.

Turning the bottle up, I downed the last swallow of the Hennessey before grabbing another and opening it. I nodded my head as Anthony Hamilton ass sung the exact words I was feeling. I was past drunk, but it wasn't enough. I must have needed something stronger because, I could still feel the emptiness that was left when Wynter walked out on a nigga. That day kept replaying in my mind and each time I found myself wanting to blow my own damn brains out. Shit was about to be on track. She had agreed to marry me and everything, but my dick got me in trouble once a fucking gain. When Wynter walked out with that nigga I thought I was in a bad nightmare that I couldn't wake up from. Her last words were what really fucked with me tough, she was married? I couldn't even be mad because I played her, but she obviously was the coach of the game. After I had a few moments to think about what was going on, I realized only one person touched that damn projector and her ass was sitting back watching the fireworks. I played that shit off because I noticed that she had her phone up and I knew that she was either on facetime or she was recording this shit. When I eased up on her ass, she was laughing with Makayla's trifling ass and I knew for sure those two were responsible for this. She hadn't even noticed me until my hand was around her fat ass neck. I snatched her fucking phone and Makayla froze up.

"Nah, bitch. Don't get quiet now. Keep laughing and when you finish, pack my daughter shit up cause I'm on the way. You next and it's going hurt my heart to tell my daughter her mom died." I spat as I turned the camera and showed her that I was choking the fuck out of the event planner, Tanya. I was watching this hoe's eyes roll into her head and still I wasn't satisfied. She was trying to say something but the grip I had on her neck wouldn't let her make a sound. *"Y'all thought this shit was funny, huh?"* I spat as I shook her.

"Bro, bro, bro you are tripping my nigga!" Shoota said running towards us. I heard him, but I wasn't seeing him. All the fuck I saw was red. I was fucking furious at these bitches but more so at myself. They wouldn't have had any ammo if I was living like I was supposed to.

"Nah, I ain't trippin yet. Just wait until I pull up on Makayla, then I'm going fucking trip." I said as I threw Tanya's bitch ass to the floor. She was coughing, gasping for air and rubbing her neck. I didn't have an ounce of regret in my body. *"Them bitches the reason I lost my shorty man. She said I could go back home and that shit was before the proposal. Nigga she said she would marry me!"* I fought back tears as I stared at Tanya on the floor.

"No Hakeem, you didn't need any help in losing your shorty. You did that on your own! I can't believe you would drag that pour girl through that when she is so close to having your baby. I'm telling you right now, don't bring your selfish ass to my house crying this time. You are on your own. And another thing, you better hope she lets me see my grandbaby. Shit like this will make the sweetest person vindictive." My mama went in on me real quick and I had nothing left to say. When

she stormed out, I noticed Koko escorting everyone out of the room too. Grabbing Shoota's gun, I snatched Tanya up by her head.

"I don't know how you knew Makayla's bitch ass to pull this shit off, but I promise this is your only out. Get your ass out of town bitch cause next time I see you will be the last time anyone sees you." I spat before throwing her back down. She quickly stood to her feet and hauled ass out the building.

"Yo?" I answered my ringing phone without looking at the call log.

"Hakeem, I'm going say this once and I won't be repeating myself again. Get your shit together and do it fast. It's barely afternoon and I can tell that you are sitting over there drinking your kidney's away. I've raised my fucking children and as fucked up as y'all are now, I did a damn good job. No one has to tell me that but, I won't be doing it again. That little raggedy ass bitch done dropped Kylie over here and pulled the fuck off as soon as I opened my door. I have her for the weekend but on Sunday night, you better come get her!" My mama screamed and banged the phone in my ear. It had been a month since that mess of a shower and she still wasn't fucking with me. Hell, I didn't want her to raise my daughter. If I wasn't fucked up, I would go over there and get her now. I missed the fuck out of Kylie and was happy that she was back. By the time I had made it to Makayla's house her bitch ass was gone. For weeks I blew up her phone and sat around her house, but it was clear that she wasn't coming back. I would have been happy about that shit had it not been for the fact that she took my fucking child. I didn't know up from down or left from right with both Kylie and Wynter missing. That shit touched a different part of my soul man. Going to my call log, I dialed Wynter's number again. I did this shit all damn day and I always got the same result, the voicemail. I had left so many damn voicemails that I single handedly filled the bitch up. I could tell she hadn't been listening to them because that shit was still full. I know she needed time to heal but her due date was approaching, and I needed to see what the plan was.

***

"Good morning ma." I kissed my mama on the cheek as she scrambled some eggs on the stove.

"You look horrible." She said, glancing my way.

"Just kick me while I'm down huh?" I replied sinking into one of the bar stools.

"Oh, I hope you didn't count on getting any sympathy from me. No sir, I'm all out of that shit." I hated talking to her ass sometimes. Her mouth had always been too damn smart, and she didn't give a damn who she was talking to, she was always raw. I often wondered if her ass could fight since she talked all that damn mouth. Not that I was trying to test that theory.

"Damn ma, I'm already going through it. Why you have to make it worse on me?" I asked as she threw, literally threw, a plate of food in front of me.

"You're going through it? That's what you just said? That can't be what you just said? I know that ain't what the fuck you just said. That you were going through it? I don't give a damn about what you're going through. You are the reason that you're going through it. I have no sympathy on you *going through it,* when I know that Wynter is going through it. That girl never signed up to be a single mother, Hakeem!" She said with her hands on her hips.

"She ain't no damn single mother ma. We just taking a break." I found myself getting pissed off at the fact that she was calling Wynter a single mother. She wasn't no damn single mother nor was she a mother who was single. There was a difference in those two and she didn't fit the bill on either of them. Fuck what her and that nigga thought they had going on, she was my fucking fiancée. Her ring was sitting on my damn pinky finger until I slipped it where it rightfully belonged.

"A break?" She asked before she fell out laughing. "Boy that girl is done with you. Try to get her to the point where she'll let you see your child and accept that for what it is. You better watch it though, cause that ass goin spread and when that stomach goes back flat issa milf!" I don't know what the fuck she knew about a fucking milf but I wasn't trying to hear none of that shit. Luckily, a distraction came.

"Daddy? Daddy!" Kylie walked in rubbing her eyes. When she realized that it was really me, she dropped her stuffed elephant and ran full speed into my arms. I was so happy to see my baby girl that it took my mind on that shit my mama was spitting. "I missed you so much!" Kylie said burying her face in my chest. Kylie was my emotional baby, so I already knew she was crying. Her lil ass cried for everything, Charlie on the other hand was a baby gangster. I think it was because Koko wasn't soft on her because she was a girl. Speaking of Koko, I grabbed my phone and facetimed her.

"What Hakeem." She answered. Her voice was dripping with anger and disgust. Like I said, everyone was at my neck over that baby shower bullshit. I guess it was because once again, Wynter cut them all off when she cut me off.

"Good morning to you too Koko." I smirked.

"I'm not laughing with you Hakeem. How could you? Charlie asks for Wynter every damn day and besides the facetime calls, we both hate that we can't see her." Koko said, shocking me. I had no idea they were even getting facetime calls.

"Oooh can we facetime Wynter?" Kylie asked. I noticed that Koko sat up and a smile graced her face.

"No way, Kylie is back?" She asked, genuinely happy. One thing I could say about Koko is that she loved Kylie like she was hers. I admired that despite Makayla's ignorance, she made sure the girls had that sisterly bond.

"Yes, it's me. I'm back!" Kylie called out. When she smiled, I realized that she was missing a tooth. Before I could ask her when she lost it, she snatched the phone to speak with Koko. It wasn't long until she asked to speak with Charlie and they were laughing like the best friends they were. Even that couldn't make me forget that Koko had been in contact with Wynter. I definitely was going to ask her ass about that. At the very least, she could tell me was Wynter still in town and was she having my baby here. I made it a daily ritual to sit outside her house for a while and see if I detected any movement, but I never did. I had so many questions to ask Koko but for now, I would enjoy the smiles on my daughter's faces. That was the only light I saw in this tunnel.

Chapter 2:

Wynter

My last tear just fell from my eyes, told myself that I wasn't going to cry no more (you did what you did, it is what it is). And that's why I walked out the door. Moved on with my life, but not really. Spent too much time wondering how could you, (you do this to us while we're in love). I guess I was thinking too much. I was thinking that the sex had your love. You never could get enough cause I kept it hot, I listen to you tell me your dreams and your fears. I wiped your tears, I was there, and this is why this is hurting me. Why her? Why her? Did I get on your nerves? Did I give you too much that you couldn't handle my love? Why her? Why her? Tell me what she was worth it, to make you put her first and deceive me.

"That should be all of it." I called out over the Monica track that was blasting from my beat pill. I wasn't in as bad of a place as I thought I would have been when I left that damn baby shower. I guess it was due to the fact that I had never stopped going to counseling so I dealt with that drama along with the rest of the shit I was dealing with. Was I hurt? Without a doubt. The thing is, when you love someone the way that I loved Supreme, and they continuously hurt you it's easy to block shit out. I blocked out the pain, the hurt and the anger by focusing on my daughter. She wasn't here yet, but I was making sure that when I brought her home she would be good. Putting tape across the box that held the last bit of Supreme's items, I felt a pain shoot through my back and knew that I was doing too damn much. "Woooo." I moaned out in pain as I rubbed my swollen belly. I was due any day now and because I took a little vacation, I was just now making sure everything for the baby was set up in my house.

"You good?" Heavy asked, coming up to take the box down. He, Koko and one of his home boys had come to help Rayne and me.

"Yeah, I think I just overdid it with that last box. I'm glad we are almost done." I said, looking down at my swollen feet.

"Yeah, shorty won't need y'all to buy her shit until she turns five." He said laughing. Rhea's room was the second biggest room in the house and we still had to use a second bedroom for some things that had overflowed. In order to help me, Rayne ended up taking the fourth room.

"That's the plan. Thank you again, for coming help me today. I don't know how I would have done this without you and Koko's help." I admitted.

"You could have called your baby daddy and his brother, and they would have done the same thing I did. I know what he did was foul and you're hurting but you know he would have made sure y'all was straight if he knew y'all were back home." Heavy said, causing me to roll my eyes.

"I knooooooow. But I still needed a little time. I'll give him a call in a minute, so he isn't blindsided by y'all dropping off his things. We have a child on the way, so we still need to talk at some point." I shrugged.

"Alright, we about to get up outta here. I'll have Rayne lock up." He said before grabbing the last box. Before he could walk out, Koko came rushing in with tears streaming down her face. "The fuck is wrong with you?" Heavy asked dropping the box and grabbing a gun I didn't know he had. But then again, what street nigga wasn't always strapped.

"Wynter, its Kylie. Remember day before yesterday I told you that she was back home?" She asked, making my heart beat.

"Yeah, what about it?" I asked, attempting to stay calm. My damn stomach and back was already killing me, so I didn't want to stress out my baby any further.

"Shoota just called, they had to rush her to the hospital." She cried out. Ignoring the pain that I was in, I grabbed a pair of Gucci slides and slipped them on. I didn't care what I looked like, I needed to make sure Kylie was fine. I loved both of those little girls with my whole heart and it would kill me if something serious had happened to either of them.

"Let's go, Rayne can drive my jeep." I said grabbing the keys and waddling my ass down the stairs.

"Ma, I'm right behind you." Heavy told Koko who immediately shook her head.

"No, you aren't. You have an important meeting baby. Go there and I will keep you updated." She said before turning and kissing him.

"Aight. Make sure Supreme knows that whatever it is, I'm praying for them." I didn't even take Heavy for the praying type. Once he and his friend hopped in his truck, we quickly filled Rayne in and then made our way to the hospital. The whole time over I rubbed my stomach. This was what I normally did to calm my nerves. Whenever I was stressed, sad, worried or uncertain, this would soothe me. In this case, I don't know what I was feeling. It would be the first time I have been face to face with Supreme since the whole catastrophe and I honestly didn't think I was ready. Nonetheless, I was on my way because this was bigger than some baby mama drama. This was about Kylie and I wanted to be there for her. I prayed that if I saw Makayla, I kept the same thought process.

"You ok?" Koko asked as we hopped out of the car and made our way to the entrance.

"I think I am." I responded. I had to keep it short because I was praying my ass off. Riding up the elevator was dead silent, we all seemed to be in our own thoughts. As soon as the doors opened, I saw Shoota, their mom and some chick I had never seen before. She was pretty and had a nice shape and all I could do was shake my head. She was sitting too far from Shoota to be here for him, so she had to be here with Supreme. Koko ran over to Mrs. Ella Mae and Rayne kept a steady pace with me. I was hoping to prolong this peace I had before they told me why we were all here but that didn't last long as I heard Supreme screaming at doctors.

"They are going to have him arrested in a moment. He has been causing all kinds of hell!" His mama cried. I knew it had to be something bad for him to give the doctors trouble. When Mrs. Ella Mae noticed me, her face lit up despite the occasion. "Wynter! Oh my God, thank God that you are here." She called out, reaching her arms towards me. I made my way to her and hugged her as best as my belly would allow. This shit had really rounded up out of nowhere. For most of the pregnancy, I barely had a pudge and now I looked like I swallowed a couple of whole watermelons.

"This is Wynter? She's prettier than he said. My name is Chelle." The chick said standing up. She had a warm smile, but I wasn't fucking with her. It had just barely made a month and the fact that she was up here cool with the family made me believe she was around before that month. Again, that wasn't the reason I was here.

"Thank you. What's going on?" I asked turning back to Mrs. Ella Mae. Before she could answer, a doctor rushed out.

"Can someone come back here and talk to him? I know that the subject is very unpleasant and that's the only reason security hasn't been called. With that being said, he cannot tear up the hospital, threaten staff and disturb other patients." He explained looking frazzled. I wanted to kick myself in the ass for not asking Koko what exactly happened before we got here.

"Wynter, maybe if he sees you it will calm him down." His mom suggested.

"Uh uh, why can't she go?" I asked pointing to Chelle. I was not ready to be thrown in a room alone with Supreme. I'm not sure when I would be ready for that shit.

"Girl, Chelle can't calm that boy down. Hell, Koko can't either." Mrs. Ella said as soon as I looked towards Koko. When I heard Supreme screaming again, I rolled my eyes and turned to the doctor.

"Lead me to the hulk." I sarcastically responded. As we walked towards the double doors, the doctor looked at my stomach.

"You sure you want to go in there while you are in that condition?" He asked showing concern.

"Yeah, I'll be fine. He's mad but he ain't crazy. He won't hurt me." I reassured him. His scary ass didn't even come in the room with me. He simply pointed to the door and damn near ran off. I softly knocked on the door twice before it came swinging open.

"WHAT'S TAKING SO..." Supreme roared but his words got stuck in his throat once he laid eyes on me. "Wynter?" He asked before I physically watched this grown ass man break in front of me. He literally shrunk in front of my face. The huffing and puffing was gone, and, in its place, I saw him battling to hold his tears back. "My baby man..." He cried out. Looking behind him, I saw that Kylie was sound asleep but there was nothing hooked up to her. No wires or anything. I stepped further in the room and he closed the door behind me. My emotions were all over the place, but my main mission was to make sure Kylie was fine.

"What's wrong with her?" I asked just above a whisper. I wasn't whispering out of fear of waking her up because she was the hardest sleeper I knew. I simply was trying to control tears of my own. I was trying to focus on her, but my heart was crying out for Supreme.

"She so young man. Not my child man, not my fucking child." He kept repeating over and over again. My mind immediately went to worst case scenario and I thought maybe it was cancer or something terminal. My ears nor my heart was ready for his next words. "Makayla let some nigga touch my fucking daughter and then let that nigga knock my daughter's tooth out her mouth when she tried to tell. My fucking baby man, and instead of coming to me." He paused as he beat his chest. "Instead of fucking coming to me and letting me handle this shit, she chose that nigga over my seed. She dropped my daughter off like she wasn't shit man. Like she was garbage!" He cried. I had never seen a man breakdown and cry like Supreme was but news like this would make the manliest of men bawl their eyes out. No one wanted their child to be the victim of a pedophile. Suddenly, our issues couldn't fit in this room, so I left them outside the door. Reaching over, I pulled him into my arms where he broke down crying. His cries shook both him and I and there was nothing I could do but be there for him. I found myself crying alongside him as I stared at the hospital bed. I would never understand how a woman can choose *anyone* over her own child. When you become a parent, you become a personal security guard, a counselor, a best friend, a cheerleader and above all you become your child's voice. To know that she confided in Makayla and instead of Makayla using her voice for her daughter to be heard, she shipped her off pisses me off.

"Uhhhhh." I moaned out as another sharp pain ripped through my stomach. Immediately, Supreme looked up.

"What's wrong? Is it the baby?" He asked.

"It's fine, I just need a seat." I said, clenching my teeth so I wouldn't scream out again. I was due in a couple days but right now, I needed to be here. As I took a seat, Supreme sat down on the cold hospital floor next to me and leaned his head on my thigh. We fell into an uncomfortable silence as we both looked towards Kylie.

"She's so fucking young man." He said aloud, more to himself than anything.

"If we have to look at the rainbow in this situation, it is

that she is so young. We have to take that negative and make it a positive. Any older and she would be tainted with this memory for her entire life. The beauty about her age is that it's rare they remember anything like this for long." I explained as he nodded in agreeance.

"Yeah, I hope you're right. When I get my hands on Makayla and that bitch nigga she's with, it's no talking. I'm not trying to hear them explain, beg or cry. They have to die for this one." He said in a calm voice. Too calm if you asked me.

"And then what would that solve? I mean yeah, they would be dead but then you would be taking away both parents from Kylie and a father from Charlie. Those little girls love you like cooked food, you have to move in ways that would benefit them and not just yourself. Think about what you going to jail for life would do to your mom, your brother, your children and Koko." I said in a low voice.

"And you? Do I have to think about you Wynter?" He asked. I wanted to ask when had he ever thought of me? When did I ever matter when it came to his decision making? When was Wynter ever taken into consideration? But then again, it wasn't the time or place. So instead of answering his question, I remained quiet. He must have caught on because he changed the subject. "You know we have to discuss Rhea, right?" He asked while touching my stomach. As soon as he touched my stomach, she kicked. Her ass must have had some big feet because it actually hurt. A genuine smile spread across his face in that moment.

"Yeah, I know. I was going to reach out to you moments before we found out you were here." I explained.

"We? Who here with you?" He asked.

"Me, Koko and Rayne. We were getting the house together when we got the call." I said.

"The house? Out here? You're moving back here?" He asked getting excited.

"I never moved away. Rayne and I just took a vacation. I needed to clear my mind and she had never left the country before so, I took her with me." I said. I thought back to how peaceful it was in the Dominican Republic. The white sands, blue water and serene atmosphere was just what the doctor ordered. It was like, as soon as I stepped off the plane, a weight was lifted off of my shoulders. Over there, I didn't have any decision to make. I didn't have any drama. It was just me and my baby girl, relaxing. Had it not been for my due date nearing, I would not be back here. The thought of having my baby in a beautiful, exotic island was inviting but despite what he did to me, I couldn't do Supreme like that. His kids were his world and he was a great father.

"You know we need to talk, right? I have so many questions..." Supreme started.

"As do I. And we will talk, when the time is right. For today, let me be here for you and Kylie." I said. He nodded his head just as the doctor walked in. I tried to step out, but he shot a look my way that said to stay put. The doctor went on to say that she wasn't penetrated, and all test had come back negative. I'm guessing they took a precaution and swabbed her for std's. The news had Supreme calm and I was happy for that.

"Thank you so much doctor. I apologize..." Supreme started before the doctor raised his hand to stop him.

"I have a daughter that is the same age as yours. Had I been in your shoes and had to sit here and endure what you have endured, I would have reacted the same way. In fact, I would have reacted a tad bit worse. It was understood. and I am happy that she is in the care of a caring parent. Take her home, smother her with love and affection, and protect your baby. I've seen so many innocent babies end up on the news because they died at the hands of a man their mother introduced them to, that I am just grateful this story was different." He said, staring Supreme in the eyes. Just the thought caused me to shudder because he was right. Just scrolling Facebook was testament of what he was saying. "I'm sure y'all are ready to leave at this point, I have your discharge papers here." He explained, handing them to Supreme as I stood to my feet.

"Appreciate ya doc. You right, I am ready to leave. I've had enough of hospitals for a while." He laughed.

"Well, I hope you have a lil bit more tolerance. We not going anywhere." I said as I looked down at the puddle of water I was standing in. it was time to welcome Rhea into this world!

Chapter 3:

Supreme

"Lord Wynter, did you just lay there and let him climb on top?" Koko asked as she held the baby of my crew, Rhea Jazelle Harris. She was truly beautiful and reminded me so much of Charlie and Kylie that it was crazy. The only difference was, I could tell this would be my first light bright child. I looked over at Wynter as she slept despite all the noise that we were making and felt horrible. She had blessed me in one of the best ways possible and all I did was bring stress into her life. That was never the plan but that's exactly what happened. Twice. For her to show up in support of Kylie reminded me of what type of woman she was. Never had I met someone so damn selfless. Most women wouldn't have shown their face at the hospital, just to spite me but she did. Then to find out that she stayed here so that I could be closer to my baby after what I did to her made me fall in love with her even more. I didn't deserve her, but I would be damn if I gave up on trying to win her back.

"Yep, he took advantage of me." Wynter mumbled. She was still high off the drugs that were administered during labor and delivery and it was funny to see her go from snoring to talking and back to snoring. Her nosey ass was trying not to miss anything.

"Lie again, Wynter!" I laughed. "I was innocent in this and you just had to take advantage of an innocent man!" The room was full of people and you could feel the love. It was so many damn people, I had to bribe the nurse not to put us out. Truth be told, it was after hours and it was only supposed to be me and Wynter in here. Looking around, I wouldn't want it any other way. I watched as Charlie and Kylie both lay on either side of Wynter and slept. You would think they worked full time jobs the way they were snoring. A nigga couldn't stop smiling when they both realized Wynter was back. They were happier to see here then I had ever seen them. It took my mama bribing their asses with food to get them to leave once it was time to deliver. When they returned, they didn't even give a damn about Rhea, they wanted Wynter and she wanted their lil asses too. While this moment felt peaceful, I knew it wouldn't last long. The whole time she was in labor, I watched her phone ring off the hook until she just powered it off. Before she turned it off, I saw Isaiah flash across the screen. That was definitely a subject we would have to visit, the two of them. I needed to know what I was up against. She surely hadn't willingly given up any information, so I would have to dig to get it out. I didn't know if they were trying to be together or if she was just on some get back shit with me. I couldn't even keep in mind that he had hurt her cause fuck, I had hurt her too. From where we stood in this race, he and I were neck and neck. He hurt her and so had I, she had my baby, but they have history and at one point she loved him past the pain he caused. With me, she was one and done. I didn't know if that was a testament to her loving him more or her loving herself more, but I knew that his ass was in for a rude awakening. Wynter wasn't the same chick he left behind.

"What you thinking about?" Koko asked walking over and sitting next to me. She must have been happy to have her girl back because this was the first time she spoke to me in weeks. At least in a nice way.

"How much I fucked up and I don't know how to fix it." I said hoping she could give me some insight.

"You can't. You hurt that girl and the only thing you can do is give her time. It's not my place but I surely told her she didn't need to think about getting back with your or Isaiah." I snapped my neck her way.

"Why the fuck would you tell her that?" I asked mugging her.

"Because, it was the truth. If you want to see that girl happy, which you should because her happiness reflects back on your daughter, you have got to let her go. Let her live her life peacefully. She has to fall back in love with herself. The two men she gave her heart to, dogged it. Then y'all both want to walk back in her life like some apology will suffice. But knowing Wynter, if the apology is big enough, she'll prematurely forgive you. And if you beg enough, she'll be foolish enough to let you in her bed, her mind and her heart again. That shit may seem like a good idea, but it ain't. She's too fragile right now and simply needs time. If you force yourself on her, the relationship won't be the same. She'll be insecure and that will cause y'all to argue and fight and eventually hate each other. Love her from a distance and be a friend to her. You didn't hear this from me, but Ice is already trying that whole friend thing. Rayne said they never really got married. I mean, they had a wedding and shit but Wynter never filed the papers. From what I hear, she burned that shit. She told him that she had some things to deal with before she decided what to do and in return, he fell back. From what I hear when I'm around her and from what Rayne tells me, he's saying all the right things to catch her in the heart. She's so broken, that at this point she's being built up on lies. You better step up to the plate. Quickly!" Koko whispered, putting me on game just ass Rhea started stirring.

"Alright Koko dang, can I hold my own damn daughter." I clowned as she passed Rhea over.

"I have to go anyway. Heavy is downstairs waiting on me. He said he couldn't come in because he been around smoke." She explained as she gathered her things. "Supreme?" She called out.

"If by some stroke of luck, she allows you in, don't do anything to fuck it up!" She warned before she walked over to Wynter and kissed her forehead.

"You leaving?" Wynter groggily asked.

"Yep, heavy is downstairs waiting for us. Congrats again boo, you have a beautiful baby and you'll be a great mom." Koko replied but Wynter had already started snoring again. Before she could even lift Charlie, Wynter was snoring again. Handing Rhea over to my mom, I motioned for Shoota to grab Charlie from Koko and I grabbed Kylie. Koko decided to bring her home with them since we were staying here. After what happened, I didn't want her out of my sight, but I trusted Koko with my life. She would never let any harm come to any of my kids. Placing the children in the car, we sat around and clowned with Heavy and Koko until I saw my mama leaving so I jogged over to her.

"You going home?" I asked, walking her to her car.

"Yeah, I'll be back with food for Wynter tomorrow but I'm tired." She explained while stifling a yawn.

"Dang, what about me?" I asked feigning hurt.

"I'm still not fucking with you. You better go up there and make it right Hakeem. That girl has been through enough and deserves the world." She said. She didn't even give me time to answer her before she hopped in her car and pulled off. I heard her and Koko, loud and clear though. After a second, I realized that Wynter was upstairs by herself and I didn't want Rhea to wake up crying, so I grabbed Shoota and went upstairs.

"So, what's your next move?" Shoota asked.

"Regarding what?" I questioned.

"Nigga. Your family. Wynter and Rhea. Y'all about to co-parent?" When he asked that I frowned up my face. I didn't even like the sound of that shit.

"Nah, I'm getting my woman back." I said as I walked into the room.

"Not while I'm alive and kicking." I saw red when I locked eyes with Wynter's pussy ass ex holding my motherfucking daughter. This day was way too fucking long.

Chapter 4:

Isaiah

This nigga was a fucking joke. Talking about he gone get Wynter back. Yeah, and my nigga where the fuck was I going to be while you rode off into the sunset with *my* bitch. Him and Wynter had me fucked up if they thought they were going to live like this was a ghetto fairytale. Wasn't no motherfucking happy ended if she wasn't with me. Holding her daughter had a nigga heart hurting. I could see a little of Wynter's features in her, like her lips and the shape of her eyes. The rest of her features came from that bitch ass nigga. This shit was borderline comical, my wife was really a mama and it wasn't because of me. She really had given this bitch nigga a fucking daughter and that shit bothered me. A nigga never believed in karma until today. She was giving this nigga everything I wanted but was too stupid to realize I could have. I don't know why I did the things I did to Wynter, I just did them. All the fucked up shit I did towards her was never a reflection of her or what she deserved. The shit I did was all on me.

"My nigga, put my fucking daughter down and we can handle this shit like men. Rhea is innocent in this shit." I could tell Supreme was trying his best to remain calm because he thought I would harm the baby, but that wasn't my style.

"Shit, she safe. I could never cause harm to a part of my wife." I said before turning and placing her back in the little plastic crib. As soon as I turned around, I was greeted by that nigga's fist to my motherfucking jaw. Flexing my shit, I was ready to give his ass the business but was interrupted.

"Supreme are you fucking serious man? My daughter is

right there! What if he would have fallen on top of her?" Wynter snapped. She tried to get out of the bed but winced in pain. I knew she was coming to grab her daughter, so I rolled the little bed over to her and handed her over.

"Stop stressing yourself ma." I said with a smile. "He hits like a bitch." I finished with a shrug. Although I wanted to tear it the fuck down in this hospital, I knew Supreme had fucked up letting her see him lose his cool. She knew I was always quick to pop off so this would work in my favor.

"I don't fucking care!" She snapped while eyeing Supreme.

"Man, how the fuck was I supposed to react to a nigga holding my child Wynter? You wanted me to shake his fucking hand. He could have hurt her just because he don't fuck with me!" he spat while mugging me. All I offered his ass was a smile.

"Oh, now you care about her being hurt? You could have hurt her all because you don't fuck with him. I heard the whole thing, he placed her the fuck down with no problems. Even said he wouldn't hurt her. I know him, he wouldn't hurt her!" Wynter argued.

"Yeah, you knew him when he was busting your stupid ass too, huh? Did that stop him from hurting your ass? You so fucking dumb behind this nigga that you just let him say he couldn't hurt something that came from you but he had no problem hurting you!" When he said that, I knew he was fucked. And from the look on his face and his brothers face, they knew it too. "I didn't mean..." He started.

"Nah, you meant exactly what the fuck you said. I'm so sick of you speaking on my fucking past and hurting me." She said as a single tear fell from her eye.

"Man, this was a fuck up. I ain't never spoke on this shit besides this time." He said. I was amused by this lil argument they were having.

"Then how the fuck Makayla knew my business to throw it in my face? Huh? How the fuck she knew that I was getting my stupid ass kicked by this nigga? Is she psychic?" She asked.

"Man, I NEVER TOLD MAKAYLA..." He screamed causing the baby to jump up and cry.

"Look what the fuck you done! If I was stupid for staying after he beat my ass I was damn sure stupid for going back to you after you cheated on me with Makayla, twice. You could have brought me something from that filthy bitch! Supreme, I want you out." She said as she tried to calm down her daughter.

"Man, I'm staying wherever the fuck my daughter staying." He said louder than necessary. Nigga was pissed off because he had this big ass vein across his forehead. I quietly chuckled but he saw it. "What the fuck is funny my nigga? You think this mean some shit, because we had a disagreement? Wynter ain't fucking with you my nigga! You can go the fuck home!" He spat again causing the baby to cry and a nurse to walk in.

"No Supreme, you can go the fuck home. I don't need all this extra stress and its obvious she was coming to say we were being too loud." Wynter said staring him in the eyes.

"It wouldn't be no fucking stress if you made that nigga leave! I ain't here to stress you out bruh. I just want to be here with my daughter. That's it." He begged.

"Should have thought about that before you called your daughter's mom stupid. You can leave." She said. As if on cue, security knocked on the door.

"We were called about a disturbance." One of them said walking in.

"Yeah, you can escort him out." She said pointing to Supreme. That nigga was turning red because he was so pissed, and I was happier than a crackhead in crack house with their next hit.

"Yo, you serious right now?" He asked her. "Man, don't do

that. I fucked up but don't do that to me." He begged.

"We can try again tomorrow. Bye." Was her response. I was happy that his punk ass lil brother followed him out and after the nurse checked her out, we were alone.

"My bad about that ma." I apologized.

"Why are you here and why did you have your hands on my daughter?" She asked while rolling her eyes. I wanted to punch her dead in those motherfuckers but then what would that solve? Instead, I released a deep breath to calm myself down before I answered her.

"I came to see you and make sure you were good." I said pointing to the bear, roses and balloons that I had got her. I had even gotten a lil bear for Rhea. "As for holding Rhea, I ain't mean no harm. I didn't think it would be a problem with me holding her because I have to get used to her at some point, right? As my wife that means she is a part of me too and I have to be around her, right?"

"I didn't say you would be around her. I never said that." She said making me side eye her ass.

"So what, every time I come over you gone send her to that nigga house?" I asked.

"*That nigga*, is her father Isaiah. And I never said you were coming over to my house. I told you that moving here wasn't a good idea." She said pissing me off.

"You said, that you didn't know what you wanted to do! You said that as of now, you didn't want to be with either of us. So, are you saying that you chose to be with that nigga?" I asked as calmly as I could. I had to shove my hands in my pocket to keep from choking her the fuck out in here.

"No, my answer hasn't changed and just because you are my husband doesn't mean you get some upper hand. I don't know what I want, but I do know I don't want to go through the things

I went through with either of you ever again. You both showed me exactly what I didn't want from my man or my relationship. I know I deserve better than I ever got from either of you, so excuse me if I decide that I just want to focus on me and my daughter. Now, if that's a problem you can leave. But hear me loud and clear, I'm not that same woman that you knew. Threatening me with my lil sister, ain't goin work because I'll die behind her and Rhea. I have no problem killing you and I would smile in my mugshot and sleep on that hard ass cot comfortably, after doing so." She spat while staring me in the eyes.

"Why you gotta bring that up man. I told you that I changed. I'm not on that shit no more. As long as I'm still fighting for something and not grasping at straws, I'm cool. Calm down killa." I laughed on the outside, but I was on fire on the inside. I didn't like this new shit she was on. Before I went to jail Wynter would try me, but I would always see the fear in her eyes. When she just said that shit to me, there was no fear. As she sat here in the hospital bed, still split open from having a child, she didn't care that I had the upper hand.

"I hear what your lips are saying, but time will reveal the truth. That is why I still say that you don't have to move here. I'm not about to make no decision in the next few days and you're not even supposed to leave Louisiana." I wasn't trying to hear shit she was saying. I was going to be wherever the fuck she was at. I wasn't getting no house here because as soon as I had her ass back, the three of us were going home. Rhea wasn't about to be around Supreme, I would raise her like she was mine. I sat around the hospital for a few hours before she asked me to leave. If she wouldn't have asked me, I was going try to sleep there. Wynter was pissing me off because she made sure I didn't touch Rhea. That shit made me feel like it was because of Supreme and how he would feel about it. On the way to my hotel, I remembered something and bust a u turn heading towards the other side of town. With traffic it took me damn near an hour to get to my destination. I didn't even knock as I bust in the house.

"Ice what the fuck bruh?" Brandon asked, jumping to his feet.

"Nigga sit the fuck down! Where yo bitch at? You sitting there telling this hoe my business and she throwing it in my gah face and shit. Makayla, bring your dumb ass out here!" I screamed. When I first found out where Wynter sent Rayne, I made Brandon come out here to watch her. I never told him to get involved with Rayne because I knew mentally, he wasn't all the way there. That nigga was worse than me when it came to putting his hands on women. I didn't even know they were together until recently, as far as I knew he was with some bitch name Makayla. All he had told me was Makayla was older than him and had a baby from some nigga that used to be big in the game but had stepped back. Makayla put the connection together before any of us did and didn't say shit. I don't even know if this nigga knew that Makayla was still fucking that nigga Supreme. He didn't pay the video at the baby shower any attention, and that would have told him all he needed to know. I sure wasn't saying shit, he beat her ass for thinking the wrong shit, he would kill her for that. I didn't even know she mentioned me to Wynter until today. I knew where Makayla got the information from to throw in Wynter's face, but if leaving her to believe that it was Supreme who pillow talked makes her push him away then that was even better.

"What you in here screaming for?" She asked walking in with an oversized t-shirt on. Makayla was a pretty chick and she was thick in all the right places, but I don't know what Brandon was thinking about trying to wife her ass. She was a hoe who fucked anything walking. She fooled her baby daddy with that "you the only nigga I'm fucking" shit and laughed about it anytime Brandon wasn't around. When she flopped down on the couch, she made sure to cross her legs slowly, so I could see her pussy. Problem was, I ain't see shit but hair. I felt my face frown up and she noticed too because she pulled the shirt down further. I was used to Wynter's pussy and she faithfully got that shit waxed. Any bitch I fucked with behind Wynter's back either was already bald down there or I made them get that shit removed.

"Why the fuck you told Wynter something about me beating her ass? That shit ain't funny and wasn't none of your business." I spat.

"Oh, that's what you tripping over? She never knew that I knew anything about you. She assumed my baby daddy told me just like I wanted her too. She still tripping on that shit?" Makayla asked while rolling her eyes. I noticed that it was cleaner than normal in here and I didn't see any toys. "I sent her to her daddy." Makayla answered the question I never asked. Brandon's phone started ringing and that nigga jumped up. I already knew it had something to do with him stalking Rayne. He thought I didn't know but the same nigga that was on his payroll was on mine, so he let me know.

"I'll be back Ice." That nigga said on his way out the door. I didn't give a fuck cause I was about to bounce too.

"You still talk to that nigga Supreme?" I asked.

"Some shit went down, and I doubt I'll ever talk to him. You still talk to that bitch, Wynter?" She asked.

"Watch your fucking mouth. Hell yeah, I still talk to her and I'm going to be talking to her. That's my rib, why you worried?" I grilled her ass.

"Not worried, I just don't see the hype behind her though." She threw her lil shade.

"Shit I don't see the pussy behind your hair. Mind your fucking business." I spat.

"Gotta dig to get to the buried treasure." She said spreading her legs.

"Ma, that shit don't make my dick hard. Close your legs and set you an appointment for a wax." I said turning to leave.

"Ice, wait! She just had a baby, so I know you need some relief." She said in a suggestive tone.

"My dick ain't going through that bush."

"Well, let me suck it." She responded while shrugging. When she licked her thick ass lips, my dick jumped. When I didn't walk away, she crawled over to me and pulled at my jeans and boxers. My dick wasn't even hard, but she smiled like a kid on Christmas morning. When my dick slipped into her wet mouth, I knew that it was wrong, but that shit felt right. No one would know about this so what was the harm in a little head?

Chapter 5:

Rayne

"I just need a break!" I said aloud as I threw the covers off of my head and sat up in bed. I wanted to cry but then what would that solve? When my phone started vibrating again, my first thought was to throw it against the wall but being that I had just gotten this one I quickly changed my mind. Instead, I powered it off and fell back onto my pillows. Why wouldn't Brandon leave me the fuck alone? The constant threats weren't even scary, it was just sick. I stayed locked up in the house with Wynter in hopes that I never had to run into his crazy ass. I knew he was back in town because one day I went to the grocery store and when I came out there was a black rose on my windshield. I knew it was him because he used to call me black rose when we first met. It was because Rose is my middle name and he said I was the first black rose he ever met. That was over two months ago, and I was still hiding out.

Climbing out of the bed, I took a quick shower and got dressed. My natural hair had been blown out and flat ironed, so it took no time for me to unwrap it. My shit was sitting in the middle of my back and I was ready to cut it. Looking in the mirror, I decided to change. I used to wear clothes that would hide my figure because I didn't want Brandon to see another dude checking me out. He was so insecure that he would whip my ass just because another nigga looked too hard. How was I supposed to control that? Even with the big ass clothes, they still looked. The only time I could dress the way I wanted to dress, is if he wanted to show me off. At times, even that would piss him off. Realizing that he was no longer my concern, I changed into a casual fit and flare dress. It was a sleeveless bright yellow dress with that hugged at my breast and stomach area and flared out from my waist. Even with the flare, my ass was noticeable. I paired it with a pair of red converse and grabbed my red Gucci backpack purse that Wynter had gotten me. No makeup was needed because I wasn't trying to sweat it off, so my nude lip gloss was all I applied before heading down the stairs.

"It's about time you got out of that room." Wynter said as she worked out to Teyana Taylor's workout dvd. To say she just had my niece a couple of months ago, her body looked better than it did before. She said it was from the breast feeding but I'm convinced that it was from waist training and the running she was doing. As soon as the doctor cleared her, she was running five miles a day and on a strict diet. The dieting stopped once she hit her pre-baby weight but not the workouts.

"I know, right?" I smiled. "Where is Rhea, upstairs sleeping?" I asked looking around.

"No, Ms. Ella Mae came and got her for the weekend. You know I kept telling her it was way too soon but today she wasn't taking no for an answer and besides, I needed to get out of this house this weekend. I'm ready for a break." She said shocking me. Wynter made motherhood seem fun.

"That can't be Wynter saying she needs a break from Rhea, huh?" I clowned.

"No, not from my baby. From her damn daddy and Isaiah's asses. They're driving me crazy and I just want to dip off without either of them knowing where the hell I'm going." She said as she wiped her face and turned the television off.

"If you would just give them the answer that they're looking for, you wouldn't have to deal with the both of them. Put one out of their misery and move on with the other. By the other, I mean Supreme too." I made it clear. I mean I know he fucked up but if she had to choose between the two, he was my choice. His fuck ups could be fixed, but once you get comfortable beating on women that shit never stops.

"It's not that simple, sis. At this point, I don't choose either of them. For once in my life, I choose me and my own happiness. I've been learning what I love and what I want and what I liked and what I disliked, in these past few months. I've been everything for everyone and for once, I'm going to be everything to myself. My baby deserves to have a happy environment. Being single, makes me happy." When she put it that way I completely understood where she was coming from. It's crazy how she got her freedom *after* having a baby. Normally, it would be the opposite. But I couldn't deny the glow that was on her face. She walked around the house singing and smiling and dancing and I never wanted that to end. I envied her because I wanted to get to that place. "What's wrong?" She inquired.

"What you mean?" I asked.

"You made this face. Like you went from smiling to borderline crying. You good?" She asked.

"I just want to be at the level of peace that you've found. I know that we were separated for some time and our bond was threatened but I have always looked up to you. Even when you thought I saw a weak woman, I didn't. I saw a woman that was too damn loyal for her own good and back then I admired that. Now, more than anything I admire that you chose the right person to be loyal too. You call the shots with both men. They can only come over when you allow, you lay all your own ground rules and you don't take shit from any of them. I love that. I want that, well not the whole love triangle thing. Just the love part." I explained.

"You know what you have to do in order to feel the love that you deserve. You know that love has been waiting for you all along, you kept avoiding it." She said and walked away. I followed her to the kitchen hoping that she would offer more advice, but she didn't. She said all she had to say.

"I'm heading out for a while, you need anything?" I asked her.

"Nah, get you something sexy for tonight though. We are going out with Koko and I'm showing off this body!" She said while making her ass clap. I laughed on my way out the house and hoped in my car to a destination unknown. All I knew was that I wanted to get some fresh air and today was too beautiful to stay in the house. Remembering what Wynter said, I made a trip to the mall and got something extra sexy for tonight before going to enjoy lunch by my lonesome. The restaurant I chose was noisy but since they had the best food, I didn't mind. Instead of complaining, I ordered my food and as soon as it came, I turned my hearing aid off. The silence gave me time to think on what I wanted to do. I had so many decisions to make but the most important one was in regard to my happiness. I never wanted to sink into that dark place I was in when I had to move here so that took priority. As I ate, I thought about when I was the happiest and found myself giggling and smiling at the memories. *"You know what you have to do in order to feel the love that you deserve. You know that love had been waiting for you all along, you kept avoiding it."* Wynter's advice replayed in my head and I knew what I had to do. Throwing money on the table, I left the restaurant with my own happiness on my mind.

"You don't know how to knock?" Shoota asked as soon as I walked into his apartment.

"If you locked your doors, you wouldn't have to worry about me just walking in. Now would you?" I smartly replied back as I took him in. He looked sexy as fuck in those grey sweatpants. He wasn't wearing a shirt and just the band of his polo boxers were showing. Against his chest lay two chains, one with his old basketball number and one with a raindrop. When he first got it made I laughed because my name wasn't even spelled like rain, but all his ass said was it was close enough. We had only known each other for two months when he got it done and I knew that he loved me even then. But still, I pushed him to the side. Then when he got "Rayne's Shoota" tatted on him, I was certain of his love for me. But still, I pushed him away. Then he stopped beating around the bush and just came out and said that he loved me. After the first time, he told it to me every chance he got. He made sure I knew that he wanted me. He told me and showed me time and time again. Still, I chose to stay with Brandon. I'm not sure if I stayed over fear, comfort or pity but I knew it wasn't love. The only man I loved was standing in front of me, looking like he wanted to push me away. The silly grin that was usually reserved for me wasn't there. The sparkle that I was so used to seeing in his eyes when they were trained on me, wasn't there either. After seeing him in the hospital, I was too embarrassed to speak and he obviously had no words for me. This would be the first conversation we had since before the baby shower.

"What you want Rayne?" He asked, before turning away from me and walking to his bedroom. I frowned at how disrespectful he was being. Although I deserved that and more, I couldn't handle it coming from him. Not one to give up, I followed behind him. Walking through his room, I realized he wasn't in there and walked over to his master bathroom. The shit was huge, and I loved how his shower was directly overhead so that it seemed as if rain was hitting your body. I watched as he adjusted the water temperature to his liking. "What do you want Rayne!" He repeated himself with more bass in his voice and hella attitude.

"You..." I whispered. I didn't expect the reaction I got from him. This nigga really laughed at me like what I said wasn't shit. "What's funny? Isn't that what you want? For me to choose you? I choose you Tre!" I repeated.

"Nah ma, I don't want shit from you. I'm good on you and all the games you play. Let yourself out." He said with no emotion in his voice.

"I'm not playing any games, Tre. I want this, I want this so bad you don't understand. It took me a while, but I finally realized that there is no place I would rather be and no one I would rather be with than here with you." I pleaded.

"I hope it don't take you as long to notice that this ain't going work in your favor. YOU DON'T FUCKING GET TO PLAY WITH A NIGGA HEART LIKE THAT!" He roared making me jump. Tre *never* raised his voice to me so hell yeah, I was scared. "You don't... You don't decide to love me when it's convenient to you. All the waiting and chasing I was doing behind you wasn't good for my health ma, a nigga ain't got no patience and I got asthma. While you were running behind that fuck nigga, I found someone that didn't come with cheat codes and shit. She knew what she wanted and went for that shit. Get the fuck out my house Rayne!" He spat before dropping his boxers and sweatpants and stepping into the shower. Running out of his room, I could barely see what was in front of me as I cried. How dare he treat me like this? He talked to me like I was nobody! I didn't even care about him try-ing to hurt me with that whole, he found someone else. He could tell that story to someone who believed him. That's not what hurt me. What hurt was how cold he was towards me. It was like he didn't give a fuck about me anymore. Opening the front door, I heard Wynter's words again. *"You know what you have to do in order to feel the love that you deserve. You know that love had been wait-ing for you all along, you kept avoiding it."* I deserved this happiness and I wasn't leaving without it. I would apologize a million times if that made him forgive me, but I wasn't leaving on bad terms. Slamming the door closed, I locked it and stripped from my clothes. I didn't even care that I was about to fuck up my blowout, this was definitely worth it. I had to calm my nerves before I went back into the bathroom because I was nervous he would reject me again. When I walked in, his eyes were closed, and he just allowed the water to rain down on him. I wasn't sure what to say, so no words came out, but I did let my mouth do the talking.

"Awww shit Rayne, the fuck is you doing?" He moaned out as I placed my hot mouth around his dick. True enough, I had only had sex with one person, but I was far from inexperienced. I watched more porn then I cared to admit and always tried the things I saw on Brandon. That was probably why his ass couldn't stay away from me. Shoota was trying to pull his dick from my mouth but I simply squeezed my jaws tighter as I continued to bob my head. Within seconds, he abandoned the task and let me make him feel better. Relaxing my throat, I eased the rest of his dick in as far as it could go before pulling it out and repeating the motion. When he started cursing and saying words I couldn't understand, I knew I snatched his soul. This was my type of apology. The spit that was falling from my mouth was mixing with the warm water that was falling over the both of us. Picking up the pace, I knew I was about to make him nut, but he wasn't ready. I saw the lust in his eyes when he pulled me up and swept me off my feet. I couldn't help the scream I let out, as his ass placed me on his shoulders so that he was eye to eye with my pussy. I was scared as hell but turned on even more. Locking my legs behind his head, I shuddered when he stuck his nose in my pussy and sniffed. I heard him release a moan before he dug in like he was starving, and my pussy was a buffet. I had no idea why I waited so long to let this happen because with just his tongue, Shoota was sending me into a high that was unmatched. I knew I would chase this type of high for the rest of my life.

"Ohhhh my God Shoota, I love you so fucking much!" I screamed out as I gripped his hair.

"I love yo ass too." He moaned into my pussy. Those words brought a smile to my face that I couldn't contain. I knew he wasn't done with me. Before I could dwell on that thought, I felt my body shaking as an orgasm ruptured through my body. You couldn't tell me that this wasn't what Heaven felt like. I could hear Shoota slurping my juices up before he lowered me down. In my mind, he was about to lower me onto my feet, but I had never been more wrong. He lowered me right onto his awaiting, rock hard dick.

"Fuck! Fuck! Shoota baby, it's too biggggg!" I whined. It had been a while since I had sex so his dick felt like it was ripping through my pussy. Plus, Shoota's dick was notably bigger than Brandon's dick was.

"Nah, you came in here being grown huh? I told you to leave but you wanted the dick, right? So, take this dick like a woman!" He roared as he stroked his throbbing dick through my wet pussy. As if I wasn't already knee deep into ecstasy, he started hungrily sucking on my neck and my breast. Once he had his fill of one area, he was back at the other area all while still shoving dick in me. Grabbing him by his hair, I pulled his face up before kissing him with enough passion to prove to him that I wanted to be here. That he wasn't an option, he was it for me. I hadn't even noticed that we were no longer in the shower until he laid me on the large countertop near his sink. Without missing a beat, he licked his thumb, and tickled my clit as he slid his dick completely out of my pussy then ramming it all the way back in. Between the repetition of that motion, his thumb and watching us through the mirror, I came so hard that my stomach started hurting. "Turn that ass over." He demanded while pulling out of me.

"I... I can't." I stammered. I wasn't lying, my damn legs were noodles. When he realized that he shot a smirk my way.

"You should have taken your ass home. Now you gon need a wheelchair because I'm just getting started. He said before leaning forward and licking from my neck down to my breast and popping one in his mouth. He slipped his dick back inside of me and I had to question myself. What the hell had I gotten myself into?

Chapter 6:

Wynter

"Take it one step further, freakum dress out my closet. Wynter filling out this skirt. I look damn good, I ain't lost it." I sang and danced in the mirror as I recorded a video to post to Instagram and Snapchat. I recently realized that I was slightly obsessed with social media and social media loved me. I had quite a few followers and was always getting direct messages asking me to model for something or the other. It was flattering but that wasn't me, I wasn't trying to be a booking info in my bio chick, this was all fun and games. Turning to the side, I swayed my hips from side to side at the Beyonce' track that was playing. All jokes aside, I was rocking the fuck out of this dress. It was a pale pink, silk Gucci wrap dress that stopped right under my ass and at the top of my thighs. It was long sleeved, collared, with a deep v neck and was belted at the waist. I was proud at how I looked in it because I worked hard to get to this size. I had gained a bit of weight thanks to Rhea, and after a lil toning it all settled perfectly at my hips, ass and breast. I went from some b cups to c cups, but I knew that wouldn't last once I stopped breast feeding. Nonetheless, I was enjoying them now as they sat on my chest like a baby's ass.

"This my songgggg!" Rayne said strutting in the room as Christina Milian's song, Dip It Low came on. We had been sipping already, so I knew she was feeling lovely. I had enough milk saved to last Rhea until I was able to pump and dump, so I was enjoying my night. I laughed as her ass started winding her hip to the words of the song. She was looking bomb in a short red romper set that hugged her thick thighs and a pair of gold cruel summer heels. I peeped how when she left here earlier her hair was bone straight but now we both had a head full of natural curls. Our faces were beat, and we were looking good and feeling better. Turning the camera her way, I recorded her on live as she danced. Hella niggas were commenting for her information but Rayne wasn't the social media type so all I let them know was that she was lil sis. "And I'm in a relationship." She added. After I ended my live I had to dig in her business.

"Since when?" I asked.

"When what?" She acted like she didn't know what the hell I was talking about.

"You left single earlier, how are you in a relationship now? Ooooohhhhh, that's why that hair messed up. You went being nasty?" I asked before moving her hair and slapping the dark red passion mark that I had just noticed on her neck.

"You told me go be happy. With Shoota, I'm happy." She shrugged. I was happy someone got their relationship affairs in order. Me on the other hand, I had issues. More issues than motherfucking vogue.

"Let's go, I'm ready." I said as I slipped my feet into the strappy stilettos that matched the pink of my dress perfectly. Grabbing a nude clutch and my keys, we made our way to my brand new G Wagon. Supreme had got it as my push gift and my God I loved it. It was dark grey with specs of purple glitter in the paint job. I knew his ass really got this to get back on my good side after I kicked him out the hospital. The next day he came back, he was kissing hella ass. Plus, he was still trying to sway my decision on our future. This shit didn't move me though, I could spoil myself and honestly, I wasn't thinking about a relationship right now. I was living life, finally. It took us no time to get to the club and it was just our luck that we were pulling up as someone up front was pulling off. I texted Koko that we were here, before we checked our makeup and hopped out the truck. Ignoring catcalls and envious stares, we bypassed the line and Heavy was waiting for us at the door. When he first said he was moving here for Charlie and Koko, I didn't fully believe him. I honestly thought he was bullshitting but he was serious as hell. This club was half his as of last week and he had already gotten a nice ass crib for them. Heavy was playing no games.

"Wassup Wynter and Rayne? Koko is this way." He greeted us with a hug before leading us through the club. Shit was lit, and I knew I wasn't bypassing that dance floor when O. T. Genasis' song, Thick started blasting through the speakers.

"I'll meet y'all up there, this is my shit!" I called out over the music before I ran to the dance floor. You have no idea how free I felt. I was never this girl, the one that was the life of the party. The one that did what she wanted when she wanted to do it. The one that was genuinely happy, all got damn day! That was never me, and I enjoyed this feeling. With my clutch tucked under my arm, I grabbed my knees and started fucking it up. I'm talking biting my bottom lip and all. When I came up, I pulled my dress down, threw one arm in the air with the other behind my head and let my ass do the rest. I didn't even object when I felt someone start dancing behind me. In fact, I made him sweat to keep up with me. I was giving him the business too and then the DJ fucked up, royally. When he threw it back to Waka Flocka song, No Hands I had a point to prove. My partner was surprisingly keeping up with me. From the arm that was wrapped around my waist, I could tell he was paid. Or borrowed someone's diamond studded Audemar watch. I knew what type and how much it was because Supreme had one exactly like this, but this guy was too bright to be Supreme. Plus, he didn't smell like Supreme. Don't get me wrong, he smelled amazing, just not like Supreme. When the song ended, I was ready to go because the DJ slowed it down and I wasn't on that shit. My partner wasn't having it though, as soon as I went to step away from him he pulled me back and spun me around to face him. When I recognized who he was, I shrugged and grinded in rhythm to him as R. Kelly sung for the DJ to slow it down. He spun me back around and pulled me close, so my ass was right on his dick.

"You look good as fuck, ma. Definitely a big change from when I last saw you." He whispered. His lips were so close to my ear that the grazed my ear when he spoke, and I could easily smell the spearmint on his breath. I couldn't even answer his ass because I think I was having an orgasm, from the damn dance. Shit, don't judge me it has been a while since I got dicked down and this was doing the trick. I felt eyes on me and looked around but couldn't find anyone noticeably staring at us. I mean people were looking, shit we were fucking it up. But not in a way that I should worry. "Look up." He whispered in my ear again. Doing as he said, I meet our real audience. My family and friends were looking down at us from the VIP area that set above the dance floor.

"Well, let's give them a show." I whispered back as I grabbed the back of his head and he pulled me even closer. This shit was so sexy that when the song ended, I damn near ran to the bar. I needed a moment to breath my own air after breathing his for so damn long. Ordering my drink, I downed it before getting another and sipping that one.

"Damn, you didn't even let me thank you for that dance." My partner said as he walked over with a smirk.

"The pleasure was all mine. I didn't know you were still in town." I replied.

"Yeah, for a few more weeks. I see you dropped your load." He smiled as he touched my now flat stomach. "You look real good." He complimented.

"Thank you, what was your name again. When you were helping me get my house situated Heavy's rude ass didn't introduce us." I said as he laughed.

"My name is Roman, but everyone calls me Ro." He answered.

"Then, I'll call you Roman because I'm not everybody. You heading up? I haven't even seen who was up there." I said, referring to the section we had for the evening.

"Yeah, I'll let you lead so I can enjoy the view." He laughed. Jumping off the stool, I pulled my dress down and made my way towards the stairs that led to VIP. When I glanced back, Roman was dead ass focused on my ass, so I made sure I swayed my hips just right. I mean if you going to have an audience you may as well put on a show.

"Damn, did y'all have on a condom down there?" Koko screamed as soon as I made it in the section. "My bitch was killing it!" She said laughing as she got up and hugged me. I couldn't do anything but laugh and blush. Again, I felt eyes on me and looked around until my eyes connected with a very pissed off Supreme. I paid him no mind as I noticed Rayne was off in the corner looking equally pissed off, so I went make sure she was good.

"What's wrong sis?" I asked.

"Oh, you didn't see the hot new couple?" She spat with fire in her eyes and venom laced in her voice. Following her eyes, I noticed Shoota had that chick from the hospital sitting on his lap. I had completely forgot about seeing that Chelle chick until this very moment and I was obviously wrong about her not belonging to Shoota. She was all smiles while he seemed to be pleading with Rayne simply with his eyes. "Oh my God Wynter, I feel so fucking dumb. I really went over there and fucked him, and he shows up with the next bitch!" She spat as tears pooled her eyes.

"Ohhhh no ma'am!" I said pulling her to her feet. "If it's one thing I've learned, is you never let these niggas see you weak! You will not cry in this bitch while he's sitting there with her ass. Look who has his attention, you do not her. I'm not saying that makes everything better but, make that nigga sweat! Make sure you show him what he is missing out on and when he comes crawling back, make it hard for his ass. Boss up boo, we ain't on no soft shit tonight." I said as I looked at Supreme again. His eyes weren't on me though. He was eyeing Roman who was eyeing me. Looking at Roman, I winked my eye in a seductive manner. I wasn't about to do anything with him, but I was going to have fun.

I wasn't getting played by niggas no more, coach may as well put me in the game because I was doing the playing from now on out.

Chapter 7:

Shoota

"Baaaaeeeeee, let's go dance like them!" Chelle annoying ass asked for the tenth time. "I'm tired of sitting around."

"Chelle, I don't dance. I didn't invite you here, so I don't see why I have to be your source of entertainment." I spat.

I was pissed off and of course I was taking it out on her ass because she was the reasoning behind my problem. Sitting here watching Rayne pop the same pussy that was just in my mouth on some nigga had my trigger finger itching. I watched her ass turn up for a few songs and was seconds from dragging her out this bitch. I knew her ass was drunk and Wynter was egging her the fuck on. They were both lit and still throwing back liquor.

It's like every fucking song that came on, her ass was shooting slugs. She stared me in the eyes as she rapped Cardi B's song, Be careful and Wynter was right there pointing and shit at Supreme. That nigga looked like he was going explode in that chair. Then as soon as Plies came on, her ass pointed at me as she screamed, "Fuck a Shoota I'm my own Shoota." Now that shit was a lil funny, but it was short lived when some nigga asked her to dance and she accepted. I know she was trying to be on some get back shit but there was nothing to fucking get back at. I ain't want Chelle ass no more and as soon as I found a way to let her ass down, I would.

"You don't have to be a fucking asshole!" Chelle spat before standing up and walking away. Getting up from where I sat, I walked over to Supreme and plopped down next to him.

"You think I'm going go to hell if I kill my baby mama?

I mean I'm already killing one, but Wynter ass about to go, tonight!" He said as he watched Wynter dance on Heavy's right hand man Ro. That nigga and Wynter had been dancing and flirting since Wynter walked in.

"I'm surprised you haven't snatched her ass up already." I said. I was serious too, I didn't think he would let it go on this long or at all, if I was being honest.

"Fuck! Cause if I go cutting the fuck up and showing my ass, she gone run! My thing is, if she would run and bring her ass back home after she got over it I would be cool. Nah, Wynter gone run straight back to that fuckboy Ice and I can't fucking have it. She going too far with this friendship thing and I think she having way too much fucking fun while I'm sitting here suffering." He spat. I really felt sorry for him because he was in a fucked up ass place.

"You do know this your fault, right? You wanted to lay down with dusty ass Makayla when you had a fucking queen waiting on your ass. Now you over here about to cry." I laughed before he turned to me and knocked my drink out my hand and turned back to Wynter. Supreme was a petty ass nigga bruh.

"You over here laughing like I don't see you in the same situation. Only difference is, I know Wynter want me. Rayne don't fuck with you like that." He said while laughing. See what I mean, petty ass nigga. Wasn't shit funny about that but because I clowned on his situation he was trying to piss me off. Nodding my head, I didn't even respond as we both sat our pitiful asses there and watched the women we love say fuck us in a whole different language.

***

"Shoota! Wake the fuck up! C'mon man, get your ass up bruh!" Before I could tell Rayne take her dumb ass back to sleep, my body hit the floor.

"Man, what the fuck is your problem?" I spazzed on her ass as I jumped up and got back in the bed. You don't wake a nigga up from some bomb ass sleep like that unless you wanted to eat a fucking bullet. She's lucky as fuck that it was her.

"My problem is that you are here, in my bed without permission." She spat before she bust out crying. "I can't believe you would use me like that." She cried as she started swinging on me. My first thought was if her ass hit so hard why didn't she give Brandon the fucking business but after seeing Wynter and Supreme go at it for that shit, I kept quiet and let her get it all out. "You let me think that we were going to be together. That something was going to come out of that shit at your house and then you show up with a bitch!" I wasn't just goin let her keep swinging on me, so I grabbed her ass up in a bear hug, pulled her onto my lap and held her as she cried. "I hate you so fucking much! You hurt me so bad." She kept repeating into my chest.

"Ma, don't say that shit. Please don't ever tell me that." I whispered in her ear. I know that this was the wrong time to be thinking with my dick, but she was sitting right on that motherfucker and she didn't have any underwear on. Even though I was bricking up, I tried to keep my mind on the matter at hand.

"I mean it Shoota! You could have stopped me if you were involved with someone. Who is she?" She asked a question I knew she didn't need the answer to. When I didn't initially answer her, she lifted her head and looked me in my eyes. "Oh my God! Is she your girlfriend? You were serious about moving on? I can't believe this shit! Why didn't you stop me before I popped your dick in my mouth?" She asked as more tears started falling from her eyes.

"Man, I told you before it even went that far. I heard the door slam and I thought you left. I didn't even know your ass was back until my dick hit the back of your throat. Even then, I tried to stop you, but you wouldn't let my dick come out of the jaws of life." I said. She had me fucked up trying to play me like I did something wrong to her ass. I didn't slide my dick in her mouth and make her suck.

"So, this is my fault now?" She asked. She was trying to get out of my arms, but I wasn't letting her ass go. She was going sit here and listen to me.

"In a way, hell yeah it is. You the one who played games with me. Man, how long have I made it clear that I wanted you? I was dead ass serious about what I said in my apartment, I don't play those type of games." I said.

"Do you love her?" She asked.

"Hell naw. We just started messing around." I honestly replied. We hadn't even been dating for a full month yet. I can't lie though, I could see me being with her for the long haul. There was something about her that made me feel like shit would be easy being with her. Her vibe was cool, and she fucked with me without me having to beg her. After chasing after Rayne for so damn long, I wanted someone that knew what they wanted and wasn't about any games.

"Then call her and tell her its over!" Rayne demanded.

"Man, what?" I laughed. That was the wrong thing to do because there were the tears again.

"I said... I said for you to call her and tell her that it's over Tre! Tell her that you want to be with me and not her! Tell her now!" Her ass said through tears. The fuck was she doing all this crying for? Even with a face full of tears, she was so fucking beautiful. Still, Chelle didn't deserve to be blindsided by all of this shit.

"Ma, I can't do that..." I started before she interrupted me.

"But I love you..." She cried out.

"Fuck, I love the shit out of you too man. I love you more than I've ever loved a female besides my mama." I confessed.

"Then why can't that be enough? Why can't us loving each other be enough for you to leave her and choose me?" She asked.

"Because us loving each other wasn't enough for you to leave Brandon and choose me." I replied back. It was as if she knew I was right because she simply nodded her head.

"I'm sorry Tre. I'm so sorry that I made that dumb decision to stay with him when my heart was here with you. I'm sorry that I hurt you and made you feel like you weren't enough for me. I choose you now and I'll choose you always. What can I do to make you forgive me for that?" She questioned.

"Give me time ma. Just give me some time to figure out how to break up with her without causing her to hurt. She don't deserve that." I said. I didn't even wait on an answer because I had waited long enough. Slightly lifting her up, I slid my dick into her wet pussy. "You goin give me some time Rayne?" I asked as I moved her hips up and down on my dick.

"Y-yeeessss." She moaned into my mouth. "I'm going give you some time." She said the answer I was praying for. At this point I didn't want to hurt either girl but I damn sure wanted them both. If that time gave me the opportunity to have my cake and to eat it then fuck it, it was a birthday party.

Chapter 8:

Koko

"You know you and Rayne showed y'all asses the other night. And then Ro didn't help the situation at all entertaining you. You know he a hoe, right?" I wasn't blocking but I had to put my girl up on game. We were sitting at my house supposed to be unpacking the last few boxes I had but instead were sipping on some wine.

"Oh girl, I can tell. His ass just knew he was coming home with me and I shut his ass down real quick. This ain't that type of party and I was just enjoying a night out with my people." She explained. I had to smile at her and this new attitude she had.

"Girl, you had our baby father pisssssseeeddddd! I could cook an egg on that nigga because he was so hot." I said laughing. "Have you talked to him since then?"

"Oh, girl you didn't hear? Him and Shoota broke in my damn house while we were sleeping. We woke up to their dumb asses chilling around like that shit was normal. Supreme wouldn't leave until I agreed to go on a date with him." She said rolling her eyes.

"Girl bye. Sitting over there acting like you don't want that old thing back. You know you miss Supreme's ass." I laughed. When she started laughing, I knew that I busted her ass trying to stunt. "When is the date? Tomorrow?" I asked

"Giiiirrrrlllll I miss that man so damn much its crazy. Whenever he comes over to see Rhea I send my ass to my room so that I don't jump on his dick and remind him who the fuck I am. Then his ass be thinking he slick, Koko. I swear to God that nigga be strolling in and enticing me and shit. I feel like I'm on that movie, Two Can Play That Game and I'm Vivica Foxx and his ass is Morris Chestnut. That nigga be walking in looking good and smelling better. He knows that I can't control myself when he gets a fresh cut and I promise you, his ass stops to the barbershop every single time he is on the way to my house!" She said making me fall out. That's some shit he would do for real though. "As for the date, his ass said he needed to make sure it's perfect so it's next week. I'm low key anxious because I thought he would have hopped on the opportunity as soon as possible. Now I need to see what the wait is for." I saw the smile on her face and noticed her eyes were staring off as she thought about him. She could say what she wanted but I already knew who she would pick.

"So, why don't you just end this whole separation thing. You're hurting yourself trying to hurt him and baby I think that falls under madness." I explained.

"Cause, I can't let him back in that quick. His ass needs to know that I mean business. Me and Rhea will be good on our own. That nigga needs to know that allllll offff thiiiisssss..." She said standing her ass on my couch and rubbing up the length of her body before slapping her own ass. "...is desirable by MILLIONS of men! I have options baby." She said popping her ass.

"If you don't get your funky ass feet off of my couch man." I said laughing and throwing a balled up napkin at her.

"Nah but for real." She said sitting back down. "I gotta let that nigga know that the old Wynter is gone. And then, I have Isaiah mixed up in this shit." She said making me roll my eyes. I hated that nigga.

"Oh yeah, I forgot your ass was married and shit." I said, side eying her ass for keeping that big ass secret.

"Girl, ain't nobody married to no motherfucking Isaiah." My eyes damn near bulged from my head.

"Wait, so you and Ice lying to people?" I asked laughing.

"Nah, just me. He really thinks that we are married but I pulled a fucking Yandy on his ass. I said, I do but those papers said, I don't as they burned in the fireplace. I wish the fuck I would get married to a nigga I physically hate. Or used to hate. Man fuck, this wine has me confused." She lied.

"Oh no, you will not blame this on the alcohol. That lil bit of wine don't have you confused, you have yourself confused. I know that you are getting back to yourself and doing you and all that good shit and I can respect that. In fact, I love this you, but I have to tell you that you are playing with fire. You have these two men that are madly in love with you and you are stringing them along. What you are doing is giving them both false hope and shit because you don't even know if you are going to pick either of them. Then you seem to be adding Ro to the already complicated equation and don't try to lie about that, I saw you two texting." I called her out on her shit.

"Why can't I just have fun? Why am I forced to choose, now? I'm not into Ro like that and he isn't into me like that. Now he, isn't getting strung along at all. Ro makes me laugh and he fine as hell but that's it. I'm not trying to fall in love with him or anything. He keeps my mind off of the craziness I deal with when it comes to Supreme and Isaiah." She explained, and I really felt bad for her. The decision seemed to be easy to me, but I have no idea of what was even keeping Isaiah in the running. He was decent looking but besides that all I ever heard about him were the horrible moments. I figured there weren't any good moments since she didn't bring them up. Maybe I was wrong.

"You're having fun at the expense of someone's heart. When you pick one, that means the other is the loser. He has to deal with the fact that instead of you just telling him what it was from the start, you made him fall deeper in love. Spending time together with them on these dates and talking on the phone, that makes a nigga fall harder than fucking him. Hell, that's going to confuse you even more. I know you said Isaiah seems to have changed, but if he did then that may have you second guessing not being with him. Then on the other hand, you love Supreme and now you have his daughter. You will have to deal with him for the rest of your life because he is a very active father." I explained.

"Yeah, yeah, yeah Oprah. I came here to hang out not to be stressed." She said rolling her eyes.

"Wrong. You came here to help me out with these damn boxes." I said pointing to the four boxes that sat in the middle of our front room.

"Oh yeah, let's do that so I can get going. But since we were talking about my situation, how are you and Mr. Heavy?" When Wynter mentioned his name, I felt that big ass goofy grin spread across my face. That shit happened anytime someone mentioned my man. "Shit, I think I got my answer from your damn smile. Bitch, I can see every tooth in your mouth. Even the back row." She clowned as she went through the boxes.

"Leave me alone Wynter! Heavy is simply amazing. From day one, he has always treated me and Charlie like we mean the world to him. For the first time in a long time, I think I'm head over heels in love. I love how Charlie loves him too. She will ask for his big headed ass before she asks for me. If he comes in late, she won't sleep until he comes to tell her good night. Like, it doesn't matter how tired she is, she will wait on him. And seeing her brings a smile on his face, instantly. He loves her just as much as she loves him. I won't even get on the fact that that man shows me in so many different ways that he is the perfect guy, for me. Let's not get on the fact that he uprooted his life in Texas, moved here and is getting out of the game. Wynter, I will body a bitch over him and not feel bad. He does that to me. With him I feel like I have everything, even if he had nothing. Without asking him or needing him to, he added me to his bank accounts. I told him I didn't need him to do that and he shut me down. He flat out told me that I was going to be his wife so what was his was mine and

Charlie's." I answered, smiling so hard my cheeks hurt.

"Awwwwww, I need a man like that." She swooned.

"You have one, make your decision." I said, sticking my tongue out at her.

"Girl, I don't mean I need a man like Heavy with money. I mean, I need a man like Heavy that doesn't cheat." She explained. "You want me to go through this box too?" she asked.

"Umm yeah, why you ask? What's in that one?" I questioned as I dug through a different box.

"Uhhhh, hold up." She said unfolding a thick stack of papers. "Bitch, I know you fucking lying." She said falling out laughing.

"What's so funny?" I asked throwing my hands on my hips.

"Girrrrlllll, I know that nigga mama didn't name him no motherfucking Hilton!" She said laughing hard as fuck. "Bitch you goin be Mrs. Hilton Manning if you marry that nigga. That's a big enough reason to say no to a proposal." She was laughing so hard tears were falling from her eyes. "Then his mama has the nerves to have a ghetto ass name like Shawnna. Why she just didn't name him Shawn?" This time when she started laughing she was on her own.

"What the fuck are you talking about? His mama name ain't Shawnna, her name is Hilda." When I said that she stopped laughing and looked at the paper again.

"He got a sister, a daughter, a niece or something?" She asked.

"Nah, he an only child and he doesn't have children. What the fuck are your reading?" I asked walking over to her. My heart was beating hard as fuck because I knew from her face that it wasn't anything good on those papers.

"Look..." She pointed. "It's him and some chick name

Shawnna Manning on damn near all these papers." I flipped through the paperwork seeing copies of a mortgage loan award letter, car titles and various other things in both of their names. I felt myself getting dizzy, so I sat on the couch. The box was obviously one of Heavy's boxes that I wasn't supposed to open. I mean, he didn't say don't open his shit, but he did tell me that he would handle his own unpacking and for me not to worry about it. Was it so that I didn't come across no shit like this? I read those papers three times before I finally spoke what was on my heart.

"I knew this was too good to be true." I cried.

"No ma'am, you not going jump to conclusions like that. You need to have a talk with him and see what's really good with this Shawnna bitch." She said snatching the papers from my hand. "Stop driving yourself crazy reading this. Wait until you two speak." She said.

"How can he explain this Wynter? One of those papers is a picture of her social security card and her ID. She's our age! I know for a fact that he has no sisters or nieces so there is only one reason a bitch his age would share his last name and have a home that was in both of their names, and all this other shit they share together. This nigga is really running game on me Wynter. This ain't no fucking typical family member sharing his name. This nigga got a fucking wife bruh!" I spat before I started crying uncontrollably. Wynter came over and hugged my shoulders. "Wynter that nigga cheating on me. I'm a fucking side bitch." I cried.

"You don't know what's going on Koko, stop being dramatic before getting all the facts." She said. For while we sat there, and she allowed me to cry my eyes out until it was time for her to go get Rhea. I was glad that Charlie was with Ms. Ella Mae because I couldn't fake like I wasn't hurting. When Heavy texted me to let me know he would be late, I had to force myself not to text him to tell Shawnna I said hey. Instead, I powered off my phone and cried myself to sleep. Loving Heavy wasn't supposed to hurt, he promised me that I wouldn't get hurt but here I am with a pillow full of tears.

Chapter 9:

Wynter

"Could you stop fidgeting, it's not like you are going on a blind date or anything, this is Supreme we are talking about." Koko said, as she put the finishing touches on my face while Rayne straightened my hair. She wasn't happy about having to straighten all of my hair just to pull it into a sleek ponytail either.

"I don't know, this just feels different. I feel like he purposely made sure that we didn't see each other over the last week. He sent either you or Shoota to get Rhea and even the text messages between us were nonexistent, unless it was about the girls. I wanted to go over and spend time with Charlie, Kylie and Rhea since they were all over there and he shut me down." I said. What I didn't tell them was how hurt my feelings were when he did that. He had never pushed me away before and this worried me. I know I said that I needed time to think about where I wanted to be, but as of lately I've only had one man on my mind. That's what made this past week hard, because he wasn't available for me. I wanted to pull a Monica and drive by his house and sit to make sure that he knew I wasn't having no fuck shit with him and any bitch, but I changed my mind. I had no rights to him and that was my fault. I wasn't even sure that we were still going to go on this date because he never mentioned it, but Koko showed up and let me know it was still on. It was a good thing I still went ahead and got my nails and feet done earlier this morning because if not, I would have been fucked.

"Isn't that what you wanted though? Space and time to think, right? If I remember correctly, it was you that said those words." Koko said making me roll my eyes.

"Who asked you, trick. You just make sure my eyebrows look like sisters and not third cousins, twice removed. How about that?" I responded. I hated that I was in the middle of the room and nowhere near a mirror, so I couldn't see the full effect of my fake ass glam squad. Koko even had a cape draped across me like she was a real make up artist. I was happy about the cape though, because I would die if any of this makeup fell on my dress. As soon as I laid eyes on it, I knew that this would be the one to make Supreme regret the way he acted this past week. The bottom was about the only thing conservative about this dress since it was fully covered and stopped right at my knees. The rest of it however, left very little to the imagination. Most of my stomach was on display and the only thing covering my breast, was barely even there. Initially, I was second guessing this because I didn't realize my breast would fill it out this way, but Koko shut that shit down and told me to just enjoy my night. After staring at myself in the mirror, I got right back on team milf. I felt extra sexy in it and I knew he would drool when he saw me in it. On my feet, were a pair of gold strappy heels and I accessorized with a gold clutch and gold jewelry.

"The last thing you have to worry about is how you'll look when you get out of my chair, trust that." She said, rolling her eyes.

Should I grab his cell, call this chic up, start some shh then hang up. Or should I be a lady, Ooh maybe cause I wanna have his babies!
Oh yeah yeah, cause I don't wanna be alone. I don't need to be on my own. But, I love this man. But some things I just can't stand oh!

"I'll be right back." Rayne said as soon as her phone started ringing. I rolled my eyes because her ass wanted to be secretive but had a whole damn ringtone set as Shoota's personal tone.

"What's going on with those two?" Koko asked as soon as she walked out of the room.

"I don't even know." I responded, with a shrug. "I hate that she is letting Shoota get over her with this whole, he needs time bullshit and I want to tell her that, so bad." I confessed.

"He is running game, why don't you tell her?" Koko asked, like it was so simple.

"Because she'll feel like I'm judging her and who am I to judge someone when my shit is fifty shades of fucked up?" I questioned.

"She will know that it is coming from love, not a judgmental place. I know you can't protect her from all this heartache, but something has to be said before it's too late. Shoota was hurt by her and you know hurt people, hurt people." She warned as Rayne walked back in. I noticed that she had cried but was sitting here trying to act natural.

"You want to talk about it?" I asked. She didn't answer me and instead started brushing my hair and securing it at the nape of my neck. When Koko handed me a mirror, I didn't even focus in on myself. I was eyeing Rayne. "You know, I'm here for you, right?" I questioned and that was all it took for her to burst out crying.

"I don't want to bother you with all this when you are supposed to be enjoying your evening, sis. This shouldn't even worry you, it's all my fault anyway." She cried with tears running down her face. My heart broke for her because I knew she was really hurting behind the situation with Shoota. She thought it was just between the two of them, but we all knew about the lil three way love affair they were involved in. Shoota was like a brother to me but he definitely had my sister fucked up.

"It's not a bother, talk." I said.

"I was soooo stupid to even agree to that stupid ass excuse

about him needing time. I'm nothing more than some late night fuck buddy. His excuse for everything is, *oh my girl this and my girl that.* FUCK HIS GIRL!" She screamed. "He can't take me out, because of his girl. He can't answer most of the time, because of his girl. He can't come over, because of his girl. I can't go to his house anymore, because of his girl. I've never been violent but Wynter I'm about to catch a case, because of his girl." She said with so much conviction in her voice that it scared me. I never wanted my sister to be, *that* girl.

"I'm not understanding, what did she do to you?" I questioned.

"She's in the way! He and I could have been happy if it wasn't for her. We wouldn't be reduced to this bullshit." She cried.

"No, that's your fault along with Shoota's fault. You wouldn't be reduced to this bullshit if you didn't agree to his offer. And you damn sure wouldn't be reduced to that bullshit had he, not reduced you to this bullshit! If he hadn't asked you to be put in this degrading position, then you wouldn't be here. It's y'all fault, she is an innocent bystander in the midst of y'all bullshit. The fucked up part is, if she falls then she will be the one left hurting in the end." I explained.

"Cough cough Ro Cough." I shot Koko a look because although she tried to disguise his name with those fake ass coughs, I heard her loud and clear.

"Rayne, you know what you have to do." I told her.

"You of all people know that decisions like these aren't easy, Wynter. If I walk away from him then I'll hurt more than if I go along with this. I love him so much that I would rather accept what he's giving me then to lose him all together." She said with a tone of finality in her voice.

"You deserve so much more than to be a man's well-kept secret." I added.

"I deserve to be happy, for once. I know that as soon as he finds a way to let her down without hurting her, we will be good. Thanks for the talk and enjoy your surprise Wynter." She said walking away. I already knew what was up at that point. She was done with that conversation and I can bet you any amount of money that she was going to be laid up with him tonight. Whenever she was like this, you had to give her some space because she wouldn't hear a word you would say. Literally, she would turn off her device and ignore your ass. I took complete blame for how down she was behind a man. Pushing her away caused her to look for love from anywhere and cling to it for dear life. This was definitely her clinging to a losing situation. Before I could dwell on the situation, there was a knock at the door. I could tell from the smile on Koko's face that she knew who it was.

"Is that Supreme?" I asked finding myself getting nervous again.

"Not yet, let's go." She said removing the cape and pulling me to my feet. She shoved my clutch in my hand and ushered me down the stairs and to the door. Swinging the door open, I was greeted by a nice looking older man holding a huge bouquet of red roses.

"Good evening, Wynter. My name is Raymond and I will be your driver tonight. The description Supreme gave of you, does entirely no justice." He said handing me the roses." I was told to allow you time to save these because, and I quote, you are extra and will want to put them in a vase on your dining room table." He said making me laugh because that's exactly what I ran to do after throwing my clutch to Koko. Returning to the door, Koko told me good night on her way out and I made my way to the awaiting Maybach. My mouth fell when I saw it because it was simply beautiful. I slid into the backseat and looked around in awe. As I rode through the streets of the beautiful city, I had an urge to snap it up for the gram. I had to take a bomb ass pic and caption it, "Boss, and I put that on my Maybach." In my Ricky

Rozay voice. But when I slid my hand into my clutch, my phone wasn't there. I knew I wasn't tripping, I triple checked my clutch before I sat down to get my makeup done and was sure I put it in the zippered part. In its place, instead of my iPhone there was short note from Koko.

Yeah, I took your phone and you better not have no nasty pictures in that bitch, or I'm uploading them to your Instagram account.

Enjoy yourself baby, you deserve all of this...

Thick ass, Koko with the big ghetto booty.

I fell out laughing because her ass just knew that she had a big booty and it was a lie. Koko was slim thick, and her ass matched her body shape, there was nothing ghetto about it. If anything, she could brag on the hips she had. With no phone to browse through, I took the time to think and enjoy the ride. There were so many reasons for me to take Rhea and Rayne and run from both of these men, but I knew beyond a shadow of a doubt, my heart would hurt without Supreme. He had hurt me and done me wrong more than once, but a part of me felt like he had learned his lesson. A part of me felt like he knew I wasn't playing games with him anymore. Then there was that other part, the part that couldn't be hurt again. I no longer had the option of falling apart once I was hurt. I now had a little human depending on mommy to get up and take care of business with a smile on her face and a pep in her step.

"Excuse me Wynter, but we have arrived." Raymond said pulling me from my thoughts. I heard the door opening and since Raymond was still in the car, my heart beat quickened, and I actually felt butterflies in my stomach. I felt my mouth form the cheesiest of smiles when I laid eyes on Supreme who looked amazing in a black, three piece suit. I had never seen him, *this*, dressed up so I was pleasantly surprised. I happily, accepted his outstretched hand and with his help stepped out of the car and into his awaiting arms. There was a weight lifted from my shoulders that I didn't even know I was carrying. This was peace.

Chapter 10:

Supreme

Avoiding Wynter for that entire week was hard as fuck but this moment right here made it all worth it. In this moment, nothing else mattered but this moment. Whatever was bothering either of us seemed so insignificant as I held her in my arms. If it wasn't for the fact that we were on a strict time constriction, I would never let her go. Stepping back, I took a look at her and knew that it would take everything in my power to stick to my plan when I wanted nothing more but to take her home and then find my way back to my home that was between her thighs. Spinning her in a circle, I knew that this date wasn't ending without us knowing what was what.

"You look beautiful." I said, kissing her cheek.

"Thank you." I was amused at this whole shy thing she was doing. I hadn't seen her blush in a while. "You clean up, *really* nice." She complimented. Wrapping my arms around her, I walked her into the space. Instead of bringing her to an overcrowded restaurant where I would have to share her with all of those people, I went a different route. There was this chef who had her own intimate dining experience, complete with staff. You had the restaurant atmosphere without the noise and crowd. Normally it was scheduled every two hours with only four clients per time slot, but I paid to have it with just the two of us. I could tell that she was amazed because her mouth dropped when we walked in. It was decorated in her two favorite colors, red and black, with roses and balloons all over. I watched her face frown up in confusion as she read a few of the balloons. "Happy Anniversary?" She read while looking my way.

"Two years ago, today, you took advantage of me in your new house ma. I should have known you were one of those fast ass little girls my mama used to warn me about when I was younger, the moment I saw you running up the street in those tight ass black shorts. I should have given you those papers and hopped in my car while I had the chance." I laughed as she playfully punched me.

"I did not take advantage of you, liar." She said, laughing. The lights above our heads hit her just right and she seemed to glow. I had to be the dumbest nigga alive to step out with a bitch like Makayla when I had someone like this, waiting at home.

"You know you raped me." I laughed. "Nah, but for real. From the moment your ass raped me, you invaded my every thought. I had plans of pulling up on your ass the next day but then you strolled into my bar with Koko and I knew it was faith. I knew way back then that though I wasn't fully ready for you, I couldn't let you slip through my fingers. A woman like you deserved the finest things in life and millions of men would cut off their right hand just for the opportunity to give it to you. With that in mind, I did everything in my power to make you mine. Then foolishly, I did everything in my power to lose you. The pain that you felt as the result of my selfishness eats me up, daily. For that reason and that reason alone, I went along with this phase you're going through. I can respect what you're doing but you need to know that when it's all said and done, this will be right where it's supposed to be." I said standing behind her and placing a necklace around her neck. On the necklace, was the engagement ring she left behind after her baby shower.

"Supreme, I'm not sure..." She started but I stopped her before she could give me an excuse.

"Wynter, I don't need you to be sure of anything because I am sure enough for the both of us. I'm sure that you trusted me with your heart and I fumbled it. Nothing I do can make that go away but I promise you, if you give me time you won't even remember that shit. Not saying that it's insignificant or anything like that. What I am saying is that I will love you to the point that you're drowning in that shit and your heart will be so full that you won't have room in it for those moments of the past. I'm not a perfect man and I never claimed to be one, but I am sure that I'm the most perfect man for you. You can search the entire world, and you still won't find the love that I have for you in anyone. It's completely unmatched because we were made for each other. Wynter, you are my rib. I'm sure that you love me and I'm sure that I love you even more than that. We have a family and those three girls love you to the moon and back and without you, our unit is incomplete. I'm sure that the things that I have done in the past, have you hesitant to let me in again. I know that, and I fully understand. But what I'm more sure of is that I can't see you loving anyone else the way you love me. I can't see me loving anyone else half as much as I love you and I don't ever want to. Life without you, ain't even worth living ma. Besides my kids, you make me whole. I need you in my life to be whole, Wynter. I get sick at the thought of you waking up to someone else. I get sick at the thought of someone making you smile, laugh, anything! I say all that to say, you may have a situation with that nigga Ice, but that ain't nothing a lawyer can't handle. My position is filled Wynter, so recruiting season has concluded, indefinitely." When I finished, her makeup was slightly messed up from how hard she was crying. Wynter was a cry baby so I knew that would happen. I was nervous because I didn't know what to expect. "Say something ma, please?" I damn near begged her.

"You hurt me so bad." She said doing the ugly cry, but still managing to be beautiful. "I was never supposed to be hurt by you, I was supposed to be safe with you!" She said, trying to cover her face. Grabbing her hands, I held them tight so that I could look her in the eyes.

"Ma, and I know it won't be an easy task for you to forgive me and to trust me again. Even with knowing I have my work cut out for me, I'm going work overtime like the rent due! There is nothing I won't do to prove to you that you are safe with me from this day forward. Me and you are a sure thing Wynter. Just give me the chance, give me one more chance with your heart. I'll work for my position, but I ain't competing. That trying to decide the winner shit is dead! I've solidified my position since the day we met. I know you still love me Wynter, by the end of this date you will be back in love with me. Go wash all that makeup off your face because you ruined it anyway." I laughed before kissing her forehead. Without another word, she walked off and I checked my phone to make sure everything was in place for the next part of the evening.

"My makeup wasn't that bad." She said returning.

"No, it was still pretty but I wanted to see your natural beauty. You wear makeup because you like it and I like it because you like it. But when it's said and done, this right here is what I love." I said pulling her close. "I tried this once before, and it went wrong. This time, I'm sure the ending affect will be more your speed." I said as a projector came on. I felt when she tensed up in my arms. "Don't trip, I'm not proposing again. Tonight." I added, and she relaxed. This time the slideshow started off with a video of all three of the girls.

"Hey Wynnie, we love you!" Charlie and Kylie said at the same time as Rhea just stared off. "Please give daddy another chance." They said, and I smirked when Wynter looked over her shoulder at me and rolled her eyes. Hell yeah, I was pulling out the big guns. If the girls would help me get back with my woman, then I was going to use their cute asses. The first picture that popped up on the screen after them was one that we took immediately after she had Rhea. Her hair was all over, she was tired, hungry and overwhelmed but I saw beauty. Rhea was on her stomach and I was on her side smiling hard as hell. Then the words Love don't change, appeared on the screen before that song started playing. She loved this song and the lyrics plus the pictures were making her emotional ass cry again.

"I got something else for you." I whispered in her ear but she paid me no mind as she sang along to the song and swayed back and forth. "Want me to sing to you?" I asked and laughed when she quickly shook her head no because my ass sounded horrible. "What about him?" I asked. She quickly looked to her left then back at the screen until she realized who she saw. Her head snapped back to the left and she jumped up and down.

"Supreme, I know you fucking lying!" She said as Jeremih walked in sing the same song that was playing on the projector.

"Wynter, my boy Supreme flew me out here because he wanted to tell you something but figured I could deliver his message a little bit better. Can I deliver his message for you?" He asked. Her ass was star struck and simply nodded her head as she leaned back into my chest. I wrapped my arms around her shoulder and smirked because this was only the beginning.

I know true love ain't easy. Wynter, he knows it's you,
'cause you complete him.
And he just don't want you to leave him,
even though he gave you reasons.

'Cause Wynter sometimes. I can tell just by your
face, this part of y'all been gone for so long. And he knows
there's no replacing what y'all had going on for so long.

But when it hurts, he can make it better. Girl if it
works, it's gon' be forever. Y'all been though the worst,
made it through the weather. Y'all problems and the
pain. But love don't change. Love don't change!

I didn't even know his ass was going add her name in it and personalize the song, but when she turned around and wrapped her arms around me I was happy as fuck. We sat there slow dancing as he sung and as soon as he finished his song, the food was rolled in. Wynter loved her food from back in Louisiana and always complained that the restaurants here couldn't come close to their flavors. It just so happened the chef was from Louisiana and had hooked up a little bit of everything. There were platters of crawfish etouffee, boudin, gumbo and all kinds of other shit I had never ate before I met her ass. After tightening Jeremih's pockets, he left with a plate and we were able to sit and just enjoy each other.

"I can't believe you did all of this, for me." Wynter said as we hopped in the back of the Maybach. I made sure the conversation at dinner stayed light because I didn't want to pressure her to make a decision. I just wanted her to enjoy the *entire* date and this was only about ten percent of what I had planned for this date.

"I'll do anything for you ma. Anything." I emphasized as she yawned. "You sleepy?" I asked.

"Yes, I'm so sorry that was rude of me. I took a nap today, so I don't know why I'm so sleepy. It's because this evening has been eventful." She said.

"Get you a light nap in, I'll wake you when we get there." I said, as she leaned her head on my shoulder. Her smile couldn't be contained although she was tired. I saw the love back in her eyes and that shit made the fact that I had to slip a sleeping pill in her drink, worth it. Desperate times, called for desperate measures. If all I had was a date to prove to her where home was, then the date would end when I said it would.

Chapter 11:

Wynter

The wind blew through my hair as I sat on the balcony reading from my kindle. I was engrossed in the pages of Crossing Lines, by this dope author name Coco Shawnde. I had gone on a reading binge of her work and she was wicked with a pen. To say I flipped out when I woke up in Turks and Caicos six days ago, I was singing a completely different tune now. I was enjoying the hell out of this *date*, as Supreme called it and I was enjoying the hell out of him too. He wasn't pressuring me to make a decision or anything, we were just basking in the moment. Sexual tension was definitely in the air, but we never acted on anything. The only problem with being here was I missed the girls. Supreme facetimed Koko for me and her and Rayne were in on the entire thing. They quickly let me know that they had Rhea and were going to get her milk wasted. Good thing I had quit breast feeding her or this trip would have been cut extremely short. Noticing a flash from the corner of my eye, I looked up just as Supreme took another picture of me.

"Come model for me." He said, pulling me up to my feet.

"Nooooo!" I laughed. "When did you get into photography?" I asked, as he continuously took pictures of me with the huge canon camera.

"I had to pick up something when my woman walked away with my heart in her pocket." He replied with a sneaky grin. "Oh, we have reservations on the beach for brunch in an hour." He said before walking off. Since I had already showered, I walked inside to see what I was wearing. When I woke up, there were bags that had everything I needed to enjoy myself from clothes, to toiletries, to hair supplies and even my correct foundation. Going into the closet, I decided to keep it simple and cute with a white cropped crotchet halter and a pair of light blue jean short shorts with a beaded brown belt. I slid my feet into a pair of brown sandals that strapped around my ankles. The sun had done my skin so well that I refused to throw makeup on it and simply applied a light layer of Mac's boy bait lip gloss. My accessories were simple, a couple of gold bangles, gold hoop earrings and a pair of oversized, gold cat eye shades. By the time I was done, Supreme was also fully dressed and we had fifteen minutes left in order to make it to brunch on time. My hair was pulled into a bun but at Supreme's request, I removed the hair tie and let my curls do as they pleased.

"We are going to be late to brunch." I observed as we walked towards the front of the resort.

"Bet $5 we won't be." He said before lifting me from my feet like I was a baby and running as fast as his legs would carry the both of us.

"Oh my God! Supreme you better not fucking drop me! Put me down silly!" I laughed. We ran past people who simply laughed or looked on in amusement at us acting like we were children. This place was so refreshing and free that they probably saw things like this often, so it didn't surprise them.

"Told you we would make it here on time." Supreme said, as he placed me on my feet. Hand in hand we made our way to our reserved seating where we placed our orders and got some drinks.

"It's so beautiful here Supreme, if it wasn't for our family I would never want to leave here." I voiced.

"We can fly out here whenever you want to ma. Just say the word and I'll make it happen for you." He said, sitting back and stroking his beard. Staring in his face, I found myself getting lost in my thoughts. My God, I loved this man from somewhere deep inside of my being. He hurt me to my core, but he also showed me real unconditional love. A part of me knew from day one that I would eventually take him back. I loved him past the hurt he caused me but before I could make a move towards being together again, I had to love myself more. I had to separate from all things that caused me pain and focus on what would make me happy. Now that I had finally put myself first, I was ready to make my move. Reaching behind me, I unclasped the necklace that was holding the ring. That ring. My ring, I guess. I noticed a look of worry on Supreme's face, but it quickly disappeared. Had I blinked, I would have missed it. I didn't address it because of course I knew why it was there in the first place.

"What's going on Wynter?" He asked, looking hesitant.

"I need to ask you something Supreme, and baby I need you not to lie to me. I'm a big girl who can handle herself so give it to me raw. I deserve the truth." I started. I know I should let sleeping dogs lie and that good shit but for me, I need to know. What... what made you cheat on me?" I asked. All the soul searching in the world couldn't give me the answer to the one question that

Chapter 12:

Ice

As I banged on the door, I thought of the different ways I would kill Wynter when I got my hands on her. She had me playing this punk ass nice guy role just for her to take me for a joke, well I was going to show her that the joke was on her ass. She forgot who the fuck I was, but I would show her soon enough.

"What Isaiah?" Rayne asked from behind the door. She hadn't even removed the chain from the door, so I could barely make out her face. I noticed her ass had the same funky ass attitude that her stanking ass sister had now. For some bitches who couldn't do shit unless I said so, they were acting real fucking brand new now. It's cool, I would humble their asses really quick as soon as I get them back to Lafayette.

"Have you heard anything from your sister yet?" I asked, if she would be rude I wasn't going to fake like this was some social call.

"I told you when she got back I would have her call you, if she hasn't called it's because she has not returned yet." She snapped. I wanted to kick that fucking door in and choke that bitch out.

"And she left her phone here?" I asked. When I first came looking for Wynter she told me that she wasn't answering because she had her phone but something about that shit didn't sit right with me. That damn phone was damn near glued to Wynter's hand at all times, so I wasn't buying this whole, she left her phone bullshit. They had me fucked up and was going to end up getting fucked up in a minute, playing around with me.

"For the third time, yes she did." She responded.

"So, you mean to tell me, your sister left for a whole fucking week, no phone and left you with her baby, and ain't told you shit about her where abouts?" I asked, while massaging my temples. I was trying hard not to spazz on her dumb ass.

"I'm almost sure that's what I said when you came here Sunday, and Monday, and Tuesday, and Wednesday, and Thursday, and Friday, and here it is Saturday and I'm telling it to you once again. I DON'T KNOW WHERE SHE IS, NOR DO I KNOW WHEN SHE IS COMING BACK!" She screamed.

"Who the fuck is you screaming at?" I snapped, unable to control my anger. "You the bitch that's hard of hearing, not me!" I didn't expect her to start laughing, but she did.

"I'm so glad my sister finally left your ass and got with a real man. What type of person threatens the woman he loves little sister to make her stay. And I'm telling you now, my phone is in my hand and I've already dialed the police. This ain't the hood and baby they come quick! My deaf ass heard that you ain't even supposed to be outside of Louisiana so try me!" I nodded my head at her bitch ass.

"You got that one ma. Maybe I should tell Brandon where your lil ass is ducked off at. I heard you wasn't half of this woman when he was putting his foot in your ass!" I spat, while kicking the door. She quickly slammed and locked the door and I knew if I kept at it she would really call the police. As I made my way to my car, I heard the door swing open and turned around.

"You know what, I do recall her saying something about her where abouts. My brother in law Supreme picked her up and showed her how bosses really roll. For a week she's been with a real nigga, sipping on the finest wines, on exotic beaches, all while getting her back blown out." When she said that shit I started making my way back to the door, but that sound of sirens made me change my mind and run to my car instead. I knew just how to humble bitches like Rayne. Speeding away, I drove to the house Brandon and that bitch Makayla were staying at and stormed in.

"Do you ever knock?" Makayla asked. She was sitting on the couch staring at her phone's screen.

"Bitch this damn near a trap house as dirty as it is in here. I wish I would show this shit some respect." I spat. She would want to shut the fuck up while my blood was boiling. I wanted to beat the fuck out of Wynter and Rayne's bitch asses, but she could fill in for them for now with the way I was feeling. "Where is Brandon?" I asked. She rolled her eyes and I had to count to ten. Bitches were so fucking disrespectful these days. That's why I never hesitated to beat a bitch down and humble her ass. That's all they need to get them to act right. Just like a puppy, they needed training and reprimanding. Shouldn't no nigga have to deal with the attitude and drama from no bitch, was my mind frame!

"Don't you have his number? Call him and ask where he is, he don't tell me his business and I don't care to ask." She said. Something in her phone must have caught her attention because she quickly sat up in her seat. Then I heard her. I know Wynter's voice from anywhere.

"What the fuck is that?" I asked her. Her eyes were watery, and she was too focused on the phone to say anything. Walking over, I snatched the phone from her hands and dared her to jump for it. The thing was, she wasn't even worried about the phone. As soon as I had snatched it, she ran out of the front room in tears. Looking at the screen, I felt my dick brick up at the sight of Wynter. Hands down my wife was the coldest woman walking the face of the Earth. She was smart, loyal, gorgeous, fine as fuck and had the tightest, wettest pussy I had ever came across. And I had come across plenty of pussy. No matter how many bitches I came in contact with, no one's pussy gripped my dick the way hers did. And I damn sure ain´t never plunged in no pussy that made me feel like my dick was gone drown like hers did. I had to smile to myself because my baby had that super soaker. Looking at the phone, I noticed that she was on Wynter's Instagram. I had searched for her on social media but always came up empty, so she used a fake name, but I read over her screen name and stored it in my head. Koldestwyntereva was real cute and described her. I scrolled her page and didn't know if I was pissed off or turned on by some of these pictures and videos. I knew this nigga Supreme was toilet paper soft. There was no way in the world Wynter would be my woman and posting twerk videos on Instagram. Nonetheless, I clicked on one. The caption said, "I gave you top of the line, I know you miss it baby".

"Fuck it up sis!" I hear Rayne's voice over the music as soon as the video started. Wynter was in these short shorts and I could tell she had either just went workout or on the way to work out from her attire.

"Girl, I'm not about to be out here doing it for the gram." She laughed and waved her off.

"One timmme, you know this your song anyway!" Rayne coaxed her, and she went for it. She turned around and started making her ass shake and clap like they made this song for her. She was dancing to this song named freak hoe and if I was in the strip club I would spend my bill money on that ass. When she dropped into a split and started popping her ass, my hand immediately went into my pants and stroked my dick. I played that damn video about ten times and still hadn't bust a nut. I needed Wynter to bring her ass home and handle this dick like only she could. Scrolling back to the top of her page, I noticed two new pictures were posted so I clicked on the first one. It was a picture of her and Rhea. She was kissing her daughter and had captioned it, "reunited and it feels so good..." I smirked because that meant she was home. Pulling out my phone, I sent her a quick text message.

Me: I've been hitting your line, I'm worried about you ma.

I was going play this good guy role just long enough for her to think shit was sweet. Knowing Rayne, she wouldn't tell her sister what happened a while ago. She wouldn't want her sister to think that she should be scared and have to watch her back from me. It was stupid logic, but in her mind, she was helping.

Wifey: Hey Isaiah, I'm good. I got away for a little while. Thanks for checking. Can we meet later on in the week? We need to talk.

Me: Hell yeah we can meet tonight, you want to come to my room?

Wifey: No! At a restaurant or something. And not tonight, I'm tired. I'll send you the info a little later.

Me: Okay ma. I missed the fuck out of you while you were gone. Rhea too.

I threw in her daughter because I figured it would give me some brownie points. If I was being honest, I didn't give a fuck about that lil bitch. The only reason I would take her when I took Wynter is because I knew it would fuck with Supreme ole bitch ass. I guess her lil trip with Supreme had let her know exactly where home was and that's why she was finally reaching out. We could have skipped the restaurant and gone straight to the room like I suggested but if she wanted to eat, I would feed her. It had been over two years since I last felt her so there was no doubt in my mind that when we did meet the night would end with her feet on my shoulders as I dug her out. My dick started to swell again as I imagined it. I was putting my face all in that pussy! Going in search of another twerk video, I remembered that other picture and clicked on it. It was a picture of her and that pussy ass nigga, in what looked like the backseat of a Maybach. When I read her caption, it was confirmed. The caption read, "I got him in the back of the 'bach, I think he catching feelings. Now it's all eyes on us, and this all lies on trust.. #offthemarket"

"Off the Market." I said aloud to myself as rage rushed through my body. That's what the fuck she thought this was? She thought she was going to break up with me when we met or some shit like that? Nah, when we said I do we said til death do us part. I wasn't some lil nigga she could just drop, I had papers on that pussy. Thinking about how she tried to play me pissed me off and before I knew it I threw the phone into the wall where is shattered into pieces. I didn't care, I was too busy trying to contain myself. I was walking back and forth like a mad man when I hear Makayla's aggravating ass voice.

"I know that wasn't my fucking phone!" She snapped. I smelled a sweet fragrance and when I turned to face her she was still dripping wet from the shower, with only a thin towel covering her body. I felt my damn hands trembling because I was pissed off, but my mind was still on Wynter and them damn videos.

"Makayla, go back in your room!" I spat. I needed time to think about the situation at hand. I needed a plan because I was getting my bitch back at all costs. If I couldn't have Wynter... Nah fuck that, it was no such thing as I couldn't have what was rightfully mine!

"What the fuck you mean, go in the room! You ain't my damn daddy and you smashed my fucking ph..." Makayla didn't even get to finish that word before I punched it right back the fuck in her mouth. I wasn't hitting her ass with all my might, but it was effective. I popped her ass in the face four times and watched as her nose stared leaking. "Oh my god!" She cried out as she took the towel that was around her body and held it to her nose. She attempted to take off running back to the room, but it was too late for that.

"No bitch, you should have gone when I told you to go!" I roared grabbing her around her slim waist. Dropping my pants, I released my dick and started stroking it. When she realized what I was doing she started shaking her head. I could tell she was a little dazed from me punching her because her reactions were delayed.

"No, please. I'm sorry!" I heard her say. It came out as a mumble because she had that big ass towel to her nose.

"Shut the fuck up. You was begging for the dick the other day and you must want it because you shaved that hairy ass pussy." I said grabbing her by her fucked up ass hair and bending her over the arm of the couch. She tried to move but I pinned her ass down while still stroking my dick so that he would get harder. I didn't even think that shit was possible. She was the one in front of me but in my head, I was envisioning Wynter being bent over. Wynter had this ass that was so fat when you bent her over, it would kind of spread on its own. Then you were gifted with the prettiest pink pussy I had ever seen. My fantasy changed for the worse when I imagined that nigga fucking *my* pussy and tarnishing it! Then my fantasy quickly turned into revenge. Wynter knew that I punished her ass when she forgot who the fuck I was. Without warning, I shoved my dick deep into Wynter's pussy. I mean Makayla's pussy. Fuck it, they were one in the same right now.

"Ahhhhh! Oh My God, please stop. You're hurting me!" She screamed. For all of that her bitch ass could shut the fuck up because all her screams did was make my dick harder. Mercilessly, I pounded into her pussy with a smile on my face.

"See what the fuck you make me do to you Wynter! You drive me crazy then get mad when I react! I don't want to hurt you, but you make. Me. So. Fucking. Mad!" I roared in between each stroke. I emptied my seeds into her pussy hopping that I got Wynter pregnant. "You goin have my baby Wynter!" I said still stroking. I knew my dick was about to get right back hard and I was ready for it.

"I'm not Wynter." She cried. Her voice was all wrong, but I was too far gone to think about that.

"Yeah, you my fucking Wynter! Why the fuck you let that nigga have what was mine?" I asked picking up my speed. Ripping my dick out of her I grabbed her hair and dragged her to the floor. "Move that fucking towel!" I demanded before grabbing her face and shoving my tongue in her mouth. She wasn't kissing me back, but I didn't give a fuck. "Suck my dick bitch!" I demanded before shoving my semi erect dick into her mouth and down her throat. I heard her attempting to talk but couldn't make out anything. In my mind, she said fuck my mouth daddy, so I did. "Open wider!" I said before fucking her throat like it was a pussy. Her mouth was so wet that the drool was landing on my balls and I loved that shit. Pulling my dick from her mouth, I sat on the couch and dragged her along.

"Ice, please stop!" She cried. Again, her voice was off.

"Isaiah! Wynter, you never call me Ice! Call me Isaiah!" I roared as I pulled her onto my lap, grabbed her hips and slammed her down on my dick with so much force I could break my shit. Hearing her scream made my nuts tickle. Yeah, she would never step out of line again.

"Oh My God! Branddddoonnn!" She screamed.

"Brandon? Wynter bitch, you just called me Brandon? You fucking that nigga too?" I roared before punching her ass in the nose again! I was seeing red and I wasn't talking about from the blood that was once again leaking from her nose. It had been so many years since I was this pissed to the point that I couldn't control myself. I hated this side of me but there was nothing that I could do. I just prayed that when I came back to the light, I hadn't killed Wynter. Her nose leaking didn't slow me up one bit because I was still fucking the shit out of her. She was getting pregnant tonight, even if she was against it. "Wynter, I love you forever ma. Remember that! Ok?" I said, but she was simply crying. "I SAID I LOVE YOU! TELL ME THAT YOU LOVE ME BACK!" I demanded with my hands tight around her neck.

"I-I lo-love you too!" She cried out just as I exploded deep inside of her pussy. Taking off my shirt, I held it to her nose and pulled her close to me.

"I hate when you make me act like this Wynter. You know how crazy you drive me. I told you that I can't let you go ma.

You are the only good in me. If you leave me, it could turn deadly for anyone that encounters you. Just be a good girl and stay with daddy. You going stay?" I asked, while rubbing her back.

"Yes." She cried out. A nigga was finally at peace, Wynter was back where she belonged. I wrapped my arms around her and lay my head back and enjoyed the moment.

Chapter 13:

Rayne

"Ok sexy mama, I see you!" Wynter cheered me on as I walked into her bedroom. I could tell she had just finished feeding Rhea and had my lil baby gone off her milk. She was sleeping like a grown woman with her mouth hanging wide open. My reason for coming in here was to pick with her before I left but I couldn't see myself disturbing her peaceful sleep.

"You always put her to sleep before I can say good night." I said fake mugging Wynter.

"Hell, her ass fell asleep on her own and I damn sure wasn't going to fight her to stay awake." She laughed as she got up to lay Rhea in her bassinet. "So, where you going?" She asked.

"On a date." I responded with a smile. I was actually excited for the dinner and a movie offer I had gotten.

"Oh yeah, with who? Shoota?" She asked, and I immediately frowned up my face at the sound of his name.

"Fuck Shoota! And when he comes over here and asks where I went, make sure you tell him I'm going make this pussy pop for a real nigga." I snapped, before storming out of her room and heading to my car. Wynter probably thought I was tripping because I never told her what happened, I was too embarrassed. Just thinking about him and how he played me last week while she was on her trip made my blood boil. The whole giving him time thing was hard as hell because I was literally sitting at home, waiting for him to find time to come and see me. I wasn't sure if he was spending all his time with his little girlfriend or in the streets, but what I did know was that barely any of it was spent with me. Despite my feelings on the situation, I knew I was wrong for how I treated him, so I accepted the little time he was willing to give. Had it been anyone else, I wasn't having it. But I was so madly in love with Shoota that I figured giving him time was nothing that I couldn't handle if the reward in the end, was to get him to myself. After having to tell myself that he was worth it one to many times it quickly became old. Anytime he realized I was frustrated with the whole thing and ready to walk away he would do something to quiet me up. This time, it was a lunch date about an hour away while his girl was at school. I was actually excited and made sure that I was dressed and made up to perfection. I had dropped Rhea off to Ms. Ella Mae and everything. I made it to the restaurant and waited and waited for him, but he never showed. To add insult to injury, I called his phone because I thought something was wrong. As soon as he answered I knew the only thing that was wrong was me. I knew he answered on an accident, he had probably rushed to ignore my call but instead he allowed me to hear him coaching that bitch on how to suck his dick. Nothing could ever prepare me for that hurt. I could handle that from anyone but Shoota. He was supposed to be my sure thing and the only thing I was sure of at that point, was that I wasn't about to sit around and be played.

"Hello?" I answered my ringing phone.

"Hey, I'm opening the garage, so you can go ahead and pull your car back." Jordan said.

"Ok, gotcha." I responded before ending the call and pulling into his driveway. When I laid eyes on him I couldn't help the smile that spread across my face. That nigga was too fine for words. The night Shoota stood me up, Jordan was having dinner with a business associate. According to him when he saw me sitting by myself looking sad, he ended his business dinner and came have to dinner with me. I enjoyed the company and it kept my mind off of Shoota. Now I definitely understood what Wynter meant when she said Ro was just around to help the time pass.

Texting and talking to Jordan made it easier for me to stop hitting Shoota up. And I guess he noticed because the roles had now reversed. I was ducking his ass like a broke bitch ducking her landlord on the fifth of the month.

"Hey beautiful." Jordan said, helping me out the car and kissing my cheek. "You look so sexy." He complimented. Since we were doing the movies, I wanted to be comfortable and still sexy. I was wearing an olive green long sleeve top, that came off the shoulders with a deep v at my breast. It was actually a bodysuit, so it was tucked tightly into my fitted, distressed fashion nova jeans. I finished my look off with a pair of camel colored heels and the matching shoulder bag.

"Thank you so much. Sorry I was late, I was too busy arguing to notice the time." I explained.

"He still taking you through the motions?" Jordan asked.

"Well now that I haven't been reaching out to him, he doesn't know how to act. He was so used to me being available at all times that this is bothering him. I took your suggestion and switched it up on him. For the past week, I've been parking my car in the garage and when he calls or stops by I don't answer. I call him back the next morning and don't offer an excuse. When he asks, I remind him of who his woman is and that she isn't me. It kills him when I say that I have no nigga to answer to." I said, proud of myself.

"Nah you didn't take all of my advice. I didn't tell your ass duck off in your house, I said bring your fine ass over here." He said licking his lips.

"Jordan, I told you that I wasn't about to stop being his fuck buddy to turn around and be yours. You made it perfectly clear that you weren't into commitments so that makes you no better than him." I reminded him.

"Yeah it do. I was upfront with my shit, you know what you are getting from me. He trying to pacify you with that time excuse just so he can have the best of both worlds." Jordan said. I noticed he was getting in his feelings and that was something that worked on my nerves about him. While I enjoyed talking to him and the distraction he provided, he wasn't a real nigga. What type of man constantly finds a reason to down talk the next man? Like cool, over drinks I opened up to him about why I was in the restaurant by myself and looking sad. From that moment forward, he would throw salt on Shoota. It wasn't like he was lying but still, why are you worried about another grown ass man. He was always comparing himself to Shoota and shit, and it got aggravating. Then whenever he mentioned us having sex, he would be butt hurt when I said no. Like nigga chill, we just met each other. I knew that this friendship wouldn't last long but for now, I accepted it. He wasn't all bad, either. It was just that his bad was outweighing his good.

"You ready to go?" I asked, attempting to change the subject.

"Yeah, let me get my keys and my coat." He said, walking away. When he slammed the door in my face instead of welcoming me in, I politely walked my ass back to my car and pulled off. I was so pissed I'm almost sure I hit his garage door. I was already accepting bullshit from a nigga that I loved but I'd be damned if I accepted that from some random ass nigga. Since I was already dressed and didn't want to go home, I headed towards the movie theater anyway. I still wanted to see Acrimony and I refused to let Jordan ruin that for me. The whole ride to the movie theater I ignored calls from him and texts from Shoota telling me I better be home tonight when he gets there. I'm going to be home just like I always am, I ain't fucking with him anymore though. Stepping out of my car, I grabbed my purse and made my way to the ticket booth to purchase my ticket. I never came to a late showing alone because it was always couples booed up and I didn't have the time to look like a lonely bitch amongst them all. On tonight, I didn't care. After getting my ticket, the smell of the nachos filled my nose and I made a detour to the concession stands. I hated that the lines were so damn long, but I got lucky today because I came twenty minutes early.

"Bae, don't you know her?" I heard from behind me but didn't recognize the voice, so I didn't pay it any mind. I heard the sound of something tapping, as if she was tapping him for his attention before she asked again. "Bae, we were at the bar with her and her sister. Her sister is Supreme's baby mama." When I heard that, I snapped my head around and mugged Shoota and his bitch.

"My sister, is no one's baby mama. And nah, I don't know that nigga." I spat, before turning back around. I was sitting in line fuming. What was the fucking chances of me running into them here? As I sat trying to calm myself down, the bitch started bothering me again.

"Excuse me, I'm sorry I don't remember you giving me your name that night we met." I spun around to face her, and she genuinely looked apologetic. Shoota on the other hand was shooting daggers at me with his eyes. "I didn't mean to disrespect you. My name is Chelle, I'm Shoota's girlfriend." She held out her hand and I remembered what Wynter had told me about it not being her fault.

"Hey, I'm Rayne." I replied.

"What are you going see? We are going to Acrimony and you can sit with us if you don't want to sit alone." She offered, and I noticed Shoota immediately looked uncomfortable. I should have fucked with his head and accepted that offer but my heart couldn't handle those type of games. I was so pissed off that they had even caught me coming to the movies by myself and found myself wishing Jordan hadn't fucked up the way he did. I didn't have to answer them, at that moment, because I was next in line. Turning around I ordered my nachos with extra cheese and extra peppers. Before I could point at the candy I wanted, God showed up and out for your girl.

"Make sure you order my popcorn bae." I heard Jordan's

voice and spun around. Shoota and Chelle both looked at him too. Shoota in anger and his bitch in lust. "Sorry I was late, someone fucked up my garage door and it wouldn't close." He explained walking over and pulling me into a hug. "I figured this was a good enough apology for my fit back at the house." He whispered, while holding me in his arms. I disagreed with him because I was getting my apology, but I would let him make it for today.

"Oh bae, this is Chelle and her boyfriend, ummmm." I snapped my fingers like I forgot his name. "Well anyway, let's go get good seats." I said completely disrespecting Shoota. Fuck him. To add insult to injury, they sat right behind us in the theatre and anytime I would lean on Jordan, Shoota's ignorant ass would kick the back of my seat. I asked Jordan to move down a few seats and ended up lying in his lap as we enjoyed the movie. My apple watch kept vibrating with texts from Shoota and I felt his eyes on me every time I ignored his ass. After a while, I just powered the shit off and enjoyed my movie.

"Taraji was crazy as hell!" Jordan said, as he walked me to my car.

"With reason. I mean yeah, she was wrong because she was listening to her sisters instead of following her own damn heart. But man, she lost so much behind him, only for him to make it and give the next bitch everything he promised her. I would snap too." I laughed.

"Well, I definitely need to stay on your good side." He joked, but that reminded me.

"Jordan, don't you need to tell me something?" I asked. How the rest of this night went, depended on how his ass answered.

"Man, you not still on that shit huh? We even, I just looked out for you." When he said that I simply nodded my head.

"Yeah, you are right. I'll let it go. I'll follow you to the restaurant." I said getting in my car. Once he pulled out in traffic and went left, I turned right. Stopping at a red light I blocked his number and made my way home. I couldn't park in the garage because Supreme's car was there and while I was happy that he and Wynter were on good terms, I knew he would rat me out to his brother about being home and I didn't want to be bothered. As soon as he crossed my mind, my phone started ringing and I knew it was him by the ringtone.

"Hello, Tre." I said, sounding as aggravated as I really was.

"Man, what the fuck type of shit are you on Rayne! You on dates and shit shorty?" I knew with all the damn screaming he was doing that he was spitting on the damn phone.

"Single women can date Tre. Can I help you with something?" I asked, ready to end the call.

"Rayne your ass ain't fucking single. Who was that nigga?"

"It doesn't matter because I'm not fucking with him anymore." I responded. "Come to think about it, I'm not fucking with you anymore neither Tre. I'm done trying with you. Your goal was to punish me for not choosing you, I get that. But when will it end? You don't even have to answer that because you're about a gallon of tears too late for me to care." I said, wiping a silent tear from my face. I was officially counting my losses with him.

"Man, chill out with all that. You said you would give me time, I just need a little bit more time ma. Look, I'm with Chelle getting some food, let me come see you after that." He said, making me shake my head.

"Ok." I said, giving him the answer, he was looking for.

"Good, I love you ma." He said.

"I loved you too." I whispered before hanging up the phone. Stepping out of my car, I ran into the house and packed me a few days worth of clothes. I was far from stupid, he wanted to come here and fuck me until I agreed with anything he said, but that wasn't happening this time. I deserved better than what he was offering but with a single dosage of dick, he would make me forget that. Making sure I locked the house back up, I hoped back in my car and made my way to a hotel. I needed some me time.

Chapter 14:

Koko

My heart was beating a mile a minute as I looked at the thick envelope sitting on the passenger seat of my car. You know how they say never go looking for something or you may just find it? Well, I went looking and I wasn't sure what I had found.

"Koko!" Wynter screamed over the Bluetooth in my car. For a second, I forgot she was on the phone.

"Huh? Yeah, wassup?" I asked.

"Girl, meet me at the Sheraton on Courtland so that I can do what your scary ass won't do. What was the point in going get all that shit printed out if you were just going to bitch up." She laughed, I heard a ding on my phone and looked at the screen to see Heavy calling me.

"Yeah, I'm on the way. Let me call you back." I said, disconnecting the call and clicking over. "Hello?" I answered with no emotion in my voice.

"Koko, where you at ma?" Heavy asked, sounding stressed.

"I'm around. I'll be home a little bit later on." I replied, not really giving him an answer.

"Yo, we good? Like the vibe between us been all off and I'm not feeling this shit. When I come home, you been making it your duty to make plans. We live in the same house and I feel like we were closer when I stayed in a different state. I just want to fix shit before it goes too far but I can't do that if I don't know what's broken. Ya feel me? Speak what's on your heart?" Heavy pleaded.

It was almost comical to me how he sounded sincere. Like he wasn't the one keeping secrets and ruining what we worked hard to build.

"No Heavy, I have nothing to tell you. We are just both very busy. I mean, I can only speak for myself when I say I have been completely open and honest with you. I have no secrets. On my part, we are good." I finished. There was a silence and I was positive it came from the venom that dripped in my voice.

"Ma, I can tell that you're feeling some type of way but speak on that shit. Why are you holding it in? Let me know what has us at each other's neck man." He pleaded.

"If I have to tell you what needs to be fixed, then baby I'm not sure if this will even work. I'll talk to you later on." I said, ready to end this conversation. Just as soon as I ended the call, he called right back.

"Nikol, I treat you with the upmost respect at all times. You are treated like nothing less than a queen by me, and by anyone while in my presence. But baby, don't ever in your fucking life disrespect me and disconnect a call when I'm not done talking!" He spoke with so much authority in his voice that it sent chills down my spine. That's what made Heavy a boss, he never even raised his voice, but I heard him loud and clear. You had no choice but to hear him loud and clear even if he whispered. He got that amount of respect out of you.

"I said, I would talk to you later." I mumbled.

"Yeah, I heard what you said and still I wasn't done talking. Be home no later than seven, Koko." He said.

"Wha..." I started but he quieted me.

"Koko, I'm not asking you. Don't make come looking for you ma. Nah tell me how much you love a nigga." He said. I didn't want to say anything to his ass, but I knew if I didn't, he would not hang up.

"I love you Heavy, see you later." I said.

"I love you too, ma. Now, you can hang up the phone properly." He responded with humor in his voice. I disconnected the call just as I pulled up to the hotel and found parking. Grabbing the envelope, I walked to Rayne's room so slow that I was damn near walking in reverse. I wasn't prepared for what may have been in the envelope, but I knew as soon as I stepped into that room, Wynter would simply get it over with. Knocking on the door, I took a deep breath just as Rayne opened the door looking a mess.

"Damn girl, what's wrong with you?" I asked.

"Nigga's ain't shit but hoes and tricks. Wynter is on her way up." She replied before hopping back in the bed. I couldn't help but to laugh at her because Rayne was so damn dramatic. Her ass was really sitting in the bed with popcorn, candy and napkins all around her as she cried to The Titanic. Who actually sits around in their feelings and chooses to watch movies that will put them deeper in their feelings? Only dramatic ass Rayne.

"Problems with Shoota?" I asked. The week Wynter and Supreme went away, she and I had tons of times to speak about what she was going through Shoota. My stance on that situation was that a nigga only did what you allowed him to and she created the monster that Shoota was trying to be. I knew for a fact that he loved the hell out of Rayne but couldn't pass on the opportunity to be with both women. Shoota was young and definitely thinking with his dick, and that never got a nigga far in life.

"Just going through the motions of being a recovering side line hoe, I guess. Wynter says I'm going through my first heartbreak and if that's the case, it'll be my last. Fuck niggas." She said, before focusing back on the television. I was happy that despite her hurting now, she was sticking to her guns. Rayne was young, so I was positive that she would love again. Hell, she was talking all this shit but if I knew Shoota like I knew Shoota, they weren't done. He was going catch his head real quick and come after his woman. Before I could tell her that, Wynter knocked on the door and I went to let her in. As she walked in, I knew something was different about her. I couldn't quite put my finger on it though.

"Hey my loves!" She called out loud as hell.

"And here go this bitch, walking in all happy and shit. News flash sis, we ain't feeling that happy shit!" Rayne called out crying. "Y'all look, tell me I'm not tripping. That bitch could have let Jack on that wood with her, huh?" She asked dead ass serious.

"Bruh, I didn't come over here to discuss The Titanic. Where is the envelope?" She asked. I handed her the envelope that I had never put down and said a quick prayer. I watched as she unfolded the papers and her eyes seemed to move extra fast as she scanned through each paper.

"I know I've been locked in this room in the dark for a few days or whatever, but I know my eyes ain't deceiving me." Rayne said, confusing the fuck out of me. I noticed Wynter use the papers to cover her face and when she did my mouth fell open.

"I know the fuck not!" I screamed jumping up and down. My own issues momentarily didn't even matter.

"Bling, bling bitches!" Wynter screamed waving her ring finger. The light reflected off of both rings and the smile on her face was huge. That's why her ass walked in glowing.

"When were you going to tell us?" Rayne asked running to her and admiring the rings.

"I don't know. We've just been enjoying it with each other first. But I will tell you that you funky baby. Go wash your ass!" Wynter answered wrinkling up her nose.

"I'm heartbroken Wynter, leave me alone." Rayne said, rolling her eyes. "See Koko, she already judging us because she's the only one with no man problems."

"Umm, wrong! Once I leave here, I have to go sit down and break up with a man who thinks that he is my husband and end a friendship before Supreme finds out and fucks me up. Plus, Supreme is going crazy trying to hunt down that bitch Makayla. He going kill her ass when he catches up to her." Wynter said, defending herself. "Girl, I have issues too. Ro will be easy, it's that damn Isaiah that will be the problem. Anyway, you ready to hear what these say?" She asked, holding the papers up. Hell naw I wasn't ready.

"Yeah, go for it." I said, before taking a deep breath.

***

Parking next to Heavy's truck I wanted to key the motherfucker, flatten a tire or three. Hell, if gas was around and it wasn't so close to the house, I would burn that big bitch down and reduce it to ashes and a frame. Instead, I angrily wiped my tears and entered the house. I smelled him before I saw him, but I wasn't ready to confront him yet. The way the living room was made, I would have to pass in front of him to get to my bedroom so that´s what I attempted to do.

"Wassup ma." He called out. I ignored his ass and attempted to powerwalk right past him. That was short lived when he didn't get up from his seat and snatched my ass the fuck back by my arm. Pulling me down to his eye level, I saw anger flash in his.

"Get your fucking hands off of me!" I snapped trying to pull away.

"Ma, I ain't no abusive nigga or nothing like that but I can remember asking you not to disrespect me ever again. Walking into my house, and not speaking is disrespectful." He said in a calm ass voice. Fuck that calm voice, I was ready to take it there.

"Does Shawnna speak every time she walks into y'all house? You know, where you pay that two thousand dollar mortgage, and the light bill, and the gas bill, and the home insurance, and the security system, and TWO CAR NOTES! Does your fucking wife, speak every time she walks into y'all house?" I asked with my vision blurry due to the tears. I let them fall but I refused to cry aloud like some bitch.

"Shit, I wouldn't know. I ain't been to that motherfucker in years." He said with a shrug.

"Wait, so you admitting to the shit? You ain't even going to explain?" I asked.

"Lie for what? Explain for what? You saw the paperwork, so you formed your own opinion about that shit without caring for an explanation. You went to your girls, and painted me out to be a bad nigga without explanation, so why you need it now? Went to the bank and dug through all those transactions already, right? So, what is left for me to explain? You got your proof." He said, waving me off like what I said didn't mean shit. Without thinking, I started swinging on his ass. You would think it was Charlie hitting him from the way he didn't flinch or anything. "Now say I let my anger get the best of me and I blackened your eye for that. Then what?" He asked.

"Why would you hurt me like this? You were supposed to be different." I broke down crying.

"Ma, I've shown and proven that there ain't another nigga like me around. You can search the world and wouldn't find another motherfucking Heavy. You can bet that. Here, since your ass a private investigator." He said grabbing a manila envelope and handing it to me. Opening it, I realized it was divorce papers from over five years ago. The date was a month after they got married.

"I don't understand. But you just recently paid all the bills on that property." I said, looking at him.

"And I will continue to do so, because I owe her that. A nigga humble enough to say, if I didn't have Shawnna I wouldn't have been at the top of the pyramid in the game. When I voiced how I wanted to jump head first into that shit, I ain't have no money for nobody to even take me serious and I never believed in getting fronted. Unbeknownst to me, when I would hit the block Shawnna would hit the pole. When it was all said and done, because of her I brought my way knee deep into the game. Before I sold my first eight ball, I promised her that I was going come up and she would never work a day in her life. I promised that if she stayed down, I would marry her ass and give her the world. As soon as I had the money, I got her the ring she deserved. Then I got arrested and I went to do my lil time. Not even two full months out of jail, I married her because I found out she was pregnant. The joke came when I found out she wasn't a month and a half like she told me, but instead she was four months. Before the ink was dry on the marriage certificate, we signed divorce papers. She kept everything, because she deserved that. Although she cheated, she was the only person who saw my vision." When he stopped, I felt so stupid. "The only thing I was wrong for and I apologize to you for, is not saying I was previously married. As for paying her bills and shit, I'm not sure if I would have ever told you because it wasn't that big of a deal to me." He shrugged.

"What if I said it was a big deal to me? I don't want you paying another woman's bills and I felt like you were being sneaky by not telling me." I expressed.

"I'm a grown ass man, I don't sneak to do shit. I don't care that you found out. If I was hiding something I would have never added you to my account. I would have just kept dumping bread in your account. As for not liking that I pay her bills, I don't know what to tell you ma. I'm not going be on some buster shit and fall back on my word because you have an issue with it. Just like if shit goes left with us, I ain't goin ever stop making sure you and Charlie good. I have nothing to hide from you Nikol, but that being childish shit ain't it. Speak what's on your mind at all times!" He said. All I could do was nod my head because I felt dumb. Before I could say anything, I heard Charlie calling for Heavy.

"When did she get here?" I asked because Ms. Ella Mae wanted her for the week.

"Her lil blocking ass called me earlier because she wanted to come home." He said making me laugh. Charlie had Heavy wrapped around her finger, which is why she called him and not me. I missed her, so I turned to go to her bedroom and kiss all over her face. Walking into her room, she ran into my arms.

"Hey, my baby, you had fun at granny's house?" I asked.

"Not as much fun as I did over here with all the balloons." She said jumping up and down.

"What balloons?" I asked.

"Come look!" She said grabbing my hand and pulling me to the dining room. When I past the living room, Heavy was no longer in there. Walking into the dining room, I knew why.

"Oh my God Heavy, stop playing!" I jumped up and down as he was on one knee in the middle of the living room that was filled with balloons and flowers. "YES! YES! YES!" I answered before he could ask.

"Nikol, I love you with my whole heart. I'll never purposely hurt you or Charlie, and I will go to the ends of the earth to protect y'all. Will you marry me, ma?" He asked me.

"Yes, she will!" Charlie answered for me. "She already said it!" She said making us fall out laughing.

"Of course, I'll marry you Heavy." I said walking closer and kissing his lips. When he slid that ring on my finger I was in shock. Who would have thought that Koko would find her happily ever after?

Chapter 15:

Wynter

Strolling into the restaurant, I looked around until my eyes landed on Roman. Since the night in the club when we danced, we had become good friends. The problem was, there was too much sexual attraction between us and I needed to end that because I was now a married woman.

"Hey beautiful." He stood to his feet and kissed my cheek.

"How are you?" I asked, while twisting my ring around my finger. I found myself doing it when I got a little nervous. I wasn't even sure of why I was nervous to do this, but I was. It wasn't like Ro didn't know what this was from the beginning. I made sure to never lead him and he seemed to be cool with what we had. We never had sex, although we spoke on it a time or two. We went on one date and even that ended up feeling like two friends. The extent of our friendship was damn near texts, facetimes and phone calls. Even with that being said, I needed to put an end to this.

"I would feel better if I didn't know why we were meeting here." He said, with a smile on his face.

"You know if it wasn't necessary, then I wouldn't even be here to bring this up. I'm back with my daughter's father, Supreme. In fact, we got married recently." I said, holding up my hand and showing him. "I say that to say this, I appreciate the friendship that we share. It means so much to me because I believe you were a huge factor in helping me to keep my head up during our break up. No matter what time I called you to cry, vent or just for a laugh you were ready and willing. You will never know how much that means to me. While I'm sad that you are leaving to go back home, I feel like the timing is perfect. I can't enter a marriage and still text single men that I have feelings for. Even if we disguised it as a friendship. I mean, I can but I choose not to." I explained.

"So, what you are saying is, you not going send me any nudes once I get home?" He asked while laughing. "I feel like its selfish of your husband to not allow that," I joined him in laughter and I appreciated him for not making this harder than it needed to be. "Nah man, for real. I wish y'all the best. You want to order some food before we leave?" He asked.

"No, Ice should be here in a minute so that he and I can have this same talk." I said already feeling a headache come along when I thought of speaking with his ass.

"Wait, I know you not trying to talk to this nigga by yourself, right? Nahhhh, you wouldn't be that damn careless." He said. The way he was looking at me made me scared to let him know that he was right in his assumption.

"But we are in a public place full of people. So technically, no, I'm not meeting him alone." I responded.

"Ma, these people will pull out a phone and record him beating your ass before they actually get off their asses and help you. Wynter, stop underestimating people. Especially a nigga like him. The only thing he has to lose is you and you're about to tell him that he is in fact losing you. At that point, he ain't got shit to lose and that makes him the worse kind of nigga. That nigga will kill you before he lets you be happy without him so even after this you going to have to watch your back ma." He warned. "Move to the table right behind me. Sit on the side so that you are looking at the back of my head. He and I will sit back to back. What time is he coming?" He asked.

"Ro, I don't want you to be involved in this. I really don't. It's not fair to you. If something goes wrong, someone will call the cops." I said.

"I'm a street nigga, so its fuck the law." He said, quoting Yo Gotti and lifting his shirt so that I could see he had not one but two guns. "Be cool ma, I got you." He said as my phone vibrated. Looking at the screen, I rolled my eyes.

"Ok, I'm about to move. He just texted me that he's pulling up." I said before swapping places. Moments later, I was looking into his eyes. "Hey Isaiah." I said, standing to my feet and giving him a hug. When I attempted to pull away, he wouldn't allow. He just squeezed me tighter.

"Damn, I miss your ass." He said, tucking his head in the crook of my neck. Again, I went to pull away just as this nigga kissed my neck and he held on tight, so I put my hand on his forehead and mugged the fuck out of him. "My bad, I got carried away." He said, making me roll my eyes.

"Whatever, you knew what you were doing. Anyway, how are you?" I asked. I was really just trying to buy time because although I was ready to officially end things with him, I wasn't ready for his reaction.

"Better, now that I'm with you." He said, as the waitress walked up and handed us menus. I grabbed mine and placed it down before looking at Isaiah who had fire in his eyes. That's when I noticed he was looking at my ring finger. I quickly shoved my hands in my lap and our eyes met. The way he was staring at me made me extremely uncomfortable and I wanted to leave, but I had to get this over with. "What the fuck is that on your finger, Wynter?" He asked with so much anger in his voice.

"That's why I asked you to meet me here. I appreciate you for being there for my sister and I when we were younger. I have no idea where I would have been had I not met you in the hospital all those years back. With that being said, we have grown apart. It was long before you went to jail but when you left, it gave me the chance to leave and spread my wings. Obviously, either of us was happy because you kept cheating and I was damn near depressed." I reasoned.

"Don't fucking speak for me! I was and still am happy with you. So, what that is? An engagement ring? How the fuck he proposed to a woman that's married. I hope you not expecting no divorce. This is for life baby." He said, while laughing.

"I don't want a divorce from you Isaiah. I am already happily married." I confessed.

"Well then if you so fucking happily married, why the fuck your dumb ass let him put a ring on your finger. Where the fuck is the ring I got you?" He asked. I realized he didn't get what I was saying.

"Isaiah, I wore that ring for maybe a week. Then you cheated, and I removed it. I'm not talking about you when I say that I'm happily married. I don't need a divorce from you because, you and I never actually got married. We went through the motions, but I never filled the paperwork." I said, feeling relieved to get it out. "Last week, I married Supreme the night before we came home. We have a child and she deserves a family." I explained.

"Bitch, fuck that funny looking child and that nigga! YOU ARE MINE!" He roared. When I noticed everyone looking our way, I knew it was time to go. Standing to my feet, I started to make my exit, but he grabbed my arm. "Where the fuck are you going. Bitch, I burned down your mama's fucking house to get you where I wanted you what makes you think I'll just allow you to walk away with no repercussions?" My mouth fell open when he said that shit and I was in shock.

"Oh she walking away, let her arm go fam." Ro said, placing one arm on Isaiah's shoulder and the other under his shirt. Isaiah must have noticed the gun also because he dropped my arm. "Get out of here Wynter." He told me. I started for the door but still heard Isaiah screaming.

"There ain't a place in the world that can keep us apart ma! I'm coming for you. You can bet that!" He screamed. I was officially spooked because he never made empty threats.

Chapter 16:

Makayla

I had no idea why both of these men were running behind Wynter, but that shit was bugging me. The bitch had my baby daddy and she had Ice going crazy as she strung their dumb asses along and I was about to put an end to all that goofy shit. She could keep Ice, I mean after the way his retarded ass snapped on me she could have him. That nigga forced me to sit there with my nose leaking and eye closing as he talked to "Wynter" about our future plans. Then when he snapped out of that delusional mind frame, he told me that he didn't apologize because I should have just gone to the room like he said. He told me to Blame Wynter for driving him crazy, not me. He wasn't the only one she was driving crazy either. Which is why my dumb ass was here, even after what he done to me. Seeing her flash a ring in her insta story, had me deep in my feelings but it wasn't like they could get married when she was still married to Isaiah. So, here I was to help Ice out, with a plan to get his bitch, all in the name of love. I was going after my baby daddy since she would finally be out of the way.

For a while I laid low because I thought he would find out what happened to Kylie but the fact that he hadn't come for me yet, gave me a little hope. Maybe she kept quiet about what happened, and it didn't really bother her. I know that the shit sounds fucked up, but I did the best thing I could do, I made sure that she was safe with Supreme. When my baby girl told me that Brandon touched her, his ass quickly denied ever being in the room with her the night before. My problem was, I never told him when and where it happened. That was of course, how I knew he was lying. Then the next day, I didn't leave her side until he left the house.

As soon as she fell asleep, I went to take a shower since I knew he would be gone all day. I was obviously wrong. When I went to check on Kylie, I walked in on the fucker punching her like she was a man. I quickly ran up on him and started swinging. When he punched me, I was so filled with rage that I ate that shit and kept fucking him up. Before I knew it, I tripped over my own damn feet and of course, his punk ass used that to his advantage. In no time, he fucked me up like I was a nigga on the street. The next day, I dropped Kylie off and hadn't seen or spoke to her since. Hell, I hadn't really spoken to anyone because I had been locked up in that damn house, up until today.

(Knock Knock Knock)

"Who is it?" I heard him call from further in the room.

"It's me, Kay." I answered.

"I don't know no fucking Kay!" He called back, pissing me off.

"Makayla nigga!" I snapped as he opened the door.

"Oh, yeti pussy." He said, laughing as he let me in. I hated his stupid ass sense of humor. The shit he said wasn't even funny, if you asked me. Just childish at best. "The fuck you want over here and how you got away from Brandon?" He asked, sitting on the couch that was in the parlor area of the suite and firing up a blunt. This nigga didn't care about any type of rules.

"I came to talk to you about Wynter." As soon as I said that bitch's name he sat up straight.

"Man, fuck Wynter! I'm going kill that bitch when I get my hands on her ass." He lied through his teeth. I could tell that he was still head over heels in love with her bitch ass.

"Look, you can do whatever you want to do with that bitch, I don't care. I just want her gone, whether it's from this state or this earth, is completely up to you. I overheard Brandon talking to his damn self. That nigga has been waiting on Rayne to come out of a hotel, so he can snatch her ass up. He plans on bringing her back to the house." I snitched.

"The fuck that have to do with Wynter's married ass?" he asked. I frowned up my face.

"Why you sound so defeated. Where is your competitive spirit? That girl loves her sister, as you already know. She'll easily traded places with her sister to make sure she's safe. As soon as you get her ass, take her far away from here. Love doesn't just die. She will fall back in love with you and I will make Supreme fall back in love with me." I said with too much damn confidence. I knew that nigga never loved me, but I would never admit that shit.

"When is this supposed to go down?" He asked, making me smile.

"Soon, I'll keep you updated." I replied getting ready to go. I didn't want to be around him any longer than necessary.

"What about some head for the road?" He suggested with a smirk on his face.

"After what you did to me, I wish you would get ran over in the road." I said before damn near running out of there. He creeped me the fuck out, but I needed him for this plan to fall into place. If I worked my plan just the way I envisioned it, Wynter, Brandon and Ice would all die in that house for the way they did me. They would regret it when it was all said and done. I was tired of people taking advantage of me and I was going to make sure it never happened again, at least not by those three. I didn't plan on raising an outside child but if raising Wynter's baby came along with getting Supreme, so be it.

Chapter 17:

Isaiah

I finally got the call I had been waiting for and a nigga was doing the dash to make it across town. I had no idea how, but Brandon's dumb ass had snatched up Rayne and had her at their house. He wanted Rayne for himself, but she was my ticket at getting Wynter back. Pulling up to the house I shook my head at this nigga. How fucking dumb were you to have her vehicle parked in your yard. She had a fucking new car that I'm positive came equipped with gps and onstar, shit that would lead the cops straight over here. I could see now that I would have to get rid of that nigga before he got me caught up. Walking into the house, I shook my head again. Why the fuck wasn't the door even locked. As I made my way into the back room, I knew why. Nigga was too busy trying to kiss on Rayne and shit. He had her in just her bra and panties, with tape over her mouth and tied to the bed while he was in bed behind her like they were cuddling. This nigga was nuts.

"Brandon nigga, who the fuck raised you? You trying to get yourself caught on a kidnapping charge?" I spat.

"What the fuck are you doing here?" He asked, trying to cover Rayne's body. Looking in his eyes, I could tell that he was on something from the glossiness I saw in them. Plus, he sounded a little off.

"I came to help your ass. Nigga are you high? Do you realize that motherfuckers can track her whip and pull up over here to arrest your ass?" I said, like I was concerned about him.

"Fuck, I didn't think about that shit. I just hopped on the opportunity. I had been waiting in that damn parking garage for days for her to come to her car and when she finally did, I almost missed her. She was digging in her trunk for something and it was the perfect time. I knocked her ass out, pushed her in and took her car and left mine." He was excited as fuck as he told me the dumb shit he did.

"Nigga, when they don't find her and call the cops they will go back to that hotel. Guess what they will find? Your fucking car and that will lead them to your dumb ass. Go swap the damn cars out!" I spat at his dumb ass.

"Can't you do it for me, I was in the middle of something."

"The fuck you been smoking nigga, dick? I don't run errands for your ass. I'll chill with her til you get back. Make sure you grab a gun in case you run into any problems." I reminded him. Nodding his head, he got dressed and we walked to the front room. As soon as he made it to the door, Makayla was walking in. She had a smirk on her face like she just knew everything was going to work in her favor.

"I'll be right back." Brandon said on his way out the door.

"You know his ass been snorting powder right?" She told me what I already knew.

"Yep, I can tell and that's what's about to get his dumb ass caught up. Where you coming from?" I asked her. When she texted me earlier she said she was home but now she stood in front of me fully dressed.

"I went pass Ms. Ella Mae house. I needed to lay eyes on my baby, I miss her so much and can't wait until all of this shit is over and I can go back to my family." She said like I gave a damn. Wasn't no way in the hell a nigga would go from a woman like Wynter to a bitch like Makayla. That was the biggest downgrade you could do. "So, what's next?" she asked.

"First, I'm getting that dumb ass nigga Brandon taken care of. His ass going get us caught up because he too pussy to take a charge on his own, but while he's high he ain't goin use his head." I explained before I picked up the phone and gave an anonymous tip to the cops about a guy in the parking garage of the Sheraton who stole a car and is armed with a gun. Black men got shot for less daily and Brandon's ass was so fucking paranoid that he would go down shooting before he went to jail. At least that's what I was banking on. My final call was to Wynter. I wasn't playing games with her ass, it was time to come home.

Chapter 18:

Shoota

When Supreme sent me an address and told me to get there asap with weapons, I asked no questions. Driving past the house like he told me to, I pulled up into the empty field and parked on side of him. Grabbing the bag from the passenger seat, I quickly moved to his car to see what the fuck was this about.

"What's going on bro?" I asked as I looked in the direction that he was looking in. The house he was staring at looked like a basic ass family house so there had to be more to it. "Who in there?" I asked.

"Bitch ass Makayla! I was going to moms to pick up the girls and I saw her speeding away from there. She wasn't even paying any attention to her surroundings, so I hit a u turn and followed her here. She lost me once she got in the neighborhood but after hitting a few corners, I saw that car. That's the one she was driving. You got what I asked you for?" He asked.

"Yeah, but I'm going handle this for you. You need to keep your hands clean, you have a family to take care of." I reminded him. Besides, it had been a while since I caught a body.

"I know I have a family, and that's why I gotta do this shit. Bro, she let a nigga touch my seed! It ain't no coming back from that shit. I wanted to ram her fucking car into ongoing traffic earlier, but I need to know who the fuck the nigga is that put hands on my daughter. So that I can put hands on him. I don't want a weapon when I meet up with that nigga, I need to kill that nigga with my bare fucking hands!" He spat, and I could only respect it.

"I feel you, but I'm coming in with you. Is there anyone else in there?" I asked.

"I don't think so. I didn't see anyone go in or come out since I been here.

"Alright, lay low for a bit. Let's just make sure, the last thing I want to do is go in there, guns blazing, and we kill an innocent person." I said.

"You right." He said sitting back in his seat. "What's on your mind? Why are you stressing?" He asked.

"Fucking Rayne man! She goin make me kill her when I lay eyes on her. It's been a fucking week and she ain't been home and refuses to answer my calls." I confessed. I was sick knowing that Rayne dead ass wasn't fucking with me. "I never expected for us to be at each other's neck like this. This shit ain't even me and Rayne." I said.

"Nigga you the reason that y'all at each other's necks. You wanted to be petty and teach her a lesson by stringing her and Chelle around. That was the dumbest shit you ever done because you can't even stand Chelle half the time. You knew you were in love with Rayne and when she came to you and confessed you should have put your pride to the side, bossed up and snatched her up. Instead, you thought like a lil nigga and lost the best woman that was in your corner. So the fuck what, it took her some time to realize she wanted to be with you. Nigga, some people go an entire lifetime and never find a love like y'all have or had. If you can't handle that girl being happy with the next nigga, you better give up Chelle and go with your sure thing." He preached.

"Yeah, I hear... Nigga, ain't that Wynter?" ?" I asked as Wynter stopped in front of the house we were watching. When she stepped out of the car, my damn mouth hit the floor when Ice walked out the house. I didn't want to jump to conclusions but when the nigga walked over to Wynter and kissed her on the lips and hugged her, and she let him, I knew then she may die in that house today.

"Nah bruh, not my... not my fucking rib bruh!" I heard Supreme say. I could tell by the tone in his voice that he was hurting. I watched the two of them walk in to the house and the door closed behind them.

"Something don't make sense though bro. Use your head real quick. I know that this shit hurts but it gotta be something more to that. For one, if she wanted to be with that nigga she simply wouldn't have married you. That was her idea to get married before y'all came back home. And two, you know she don't fuck with Makayla. I can bet you any amount of money that her ass don't even know Makayla in there." I said. Wasn't no way she willingly chilling with Makayla. Wynter wasn't no fucking snake.

"I guess we about to find out. Let's go." Supreme said grabbing one of the guns with the silencers and jumping out of the car before making his way up the street. With no hesitation, I followed. Easing up to the door, we heard what sounded like fighting.

"I told your ass!" I said before Supreme kicked the door of the fucking hinges. This nigga turned into Hulk behind his wife. Rushing in the front door, we saw Wynter fucking Makayla up, but Ice wasn't in the room. When she looked up at us, I saw relief flash across her face.

"He. In. The. Room. Go. Get. Rayne." She said in between punches to Makayla's face. "You let a nigga touch my baby bitch!" She screamed before it registered to me what she said, and I took off down the hallway. Looking in each room, I came up empty until I got to the last one.

"Put that fucking gun down before I snap this bitch neck!" Ice screamed. Rayne had tears running down her cheeks as Ice held her from behind with his arm around her neck. When I saw his grip tighten on her neck, I threw the gun down.

"My nigga, that's a female. Fight me if you have an issue, why include her in this shit." I said anything to get him to let her go.

"This shit ain't about you or that bitch ass brother of yours. I WANT MY BITCH! GO GET ME WYNTER NOW!" He screamed and all I noticed was his grip tightening. I didn't want to leave Rayne, but I didn't want this nigga to keep squeezing either. I heard footsteps and then Wynter walked in still out of breath.

"Ice baby, my sister don't have shit to do with you and I. Let her go and we can talk about this." She spoke calmly. You could tell they had been down this road before.

"There is nothing to talk about. If I can't be happy with you then you can't be happy without me ma. Killing you would be too easy. I'll hurt you more if let you live knowing that you're the reason your sister ain't here." He told her. I wanted to react to that shit but I realized that as long as they were talking, his grip loosened.

"Ok, then we will be together. I can't let you kill my sister. I'll go back home with you. Today, now!" She said before turning to me. "Tell your brother, that I'm sorry but this isn't going to work out. I'm goin back home with Isaiah." She said handing me her wedding rings.

"What the fuck, Wynter no bruh!" I said.

"Shut the fuck up!" Ice told me. "Wynter was and will always be mine. Come here Wynter. Once you come here, then I'll let her go and they can leave! Then it can be just the two of us, like it's supposed to be." She nodded her head and walked over to them and like he said, he let Rayne go. Rayne ran into Wynter's arms and cried for her not to leave with him. But Wynter kept repeating that she had to. When she winked at Rayne it hit me that Supreme's ass wasn't in here. I knew they had something up their sleeves, so I grabbed a crying Rayne and walked out. Ice's ass was smiling so big you would think he won the power ball. Taking another look in the room, I noticed he didn't even care that we were still in the house before he had her pinned against the wall kissing her. Leaving his back to the door. When I saw Supreme in the hallway, I realized that was the plan. There was no gunshot heard, because while Wynter kept him preoccupied, Supreme snuck up behind Ice and snapped his neck just as he had threatened to do to Rayne's.

"You good ma?" I asked her. She never answered me though, she was just staring ahead. I noticed she had dry blood in the back of her hair and it looked like she was hit over the head with something. I'm not sure if she was in shock from what just happened or if she was suffering from the blow to the head but I was happy that she was alive and I had a chance to make things right.

**

Sitting next to Rayne as she lay hooked up to all kinds of machines, my heart was beating a mile a minute. Everyone seemed to be relaxed and at peace with what went down but all that kept running through my head was how I almost lost my shorty. Both of them. To get to the hospital and find out that Rayne was pregnant with my seed lit a fire under my ass. As we all sat around the hospital room, a news story came on that left our mouths hanging. Brandon's bitch ass had gotten shot and killed by the police after waiving a gun at them. He was in Rayne's car when the shit went down.

"Bitch ass nigga, got off lucky!" Supreme spat.

"Am I missing something?" I asked him. I knew why I didn't like the nigga but Supreme seemed more pissed than me.

"Before Makayla umm, passed away, she said Brandon was the guy who touched Kylie." Wynter said, shaking her head. I still couldn't believe Wynter's lil ass beat Makayla to death. That was some reserved ass anger. No one knew what went down in that house besides us because on our way out, we torched that bitch.

"Ma, you never gave me an answer." I said, leaning over to

whisper in Rayne's ear.

"Shoota if your ugly ass can try me like that again, I'll kill you and the bitch. On my child! Yeah, I'm rocking with you boy. Don't make me regret it." She said making a nigga smile. I shot a quick text to Chelle telling her it was over and then blocked her number. Fuck worrying about her feelings, if my baby was cool then so was I.

The End

Sad to see the story end? Trenae' has a collection of other juicy stories for you to indulge in! Head on over to Amazon to one click or get them for free with Kindle Unlimited today!

The Sins of my Beretta 1

The Sins of my Beretta 2

You Gon' Pay Me with Tears 1

You Gon' Pay Me with Tears 2

The Sins of my Beretta 3

Wishing He Was My Savage 1

Wishing He Was My Savage 2

Wishing He Was My Savage 3

Dynastii & Tec (Standalone)

Wynter: An Ice-Cold Love 1

Wynter: An Ice-Cold Love 2

Promised to A Boss

Promised to A Boss 2

Thick Thighs Save Lives (Anthology)

If Only You Knew: A Novella

Made in the USA
Columbia, SC
05 September 2020

19632981R00074